THE DIREWOLF OF MURKFELL

H.R. PARKER

Edited by
S.R MALONE

NIGHTWILD

PRESS

You are the light in the darkness

INTRODUCTION

My earliest lore began with fairy tales.

The real deal—Perrault, Grimm, Andersen—not the watered-down, sugary-sweet Disney versions. Dark forests that harbor even darker secrets. Cannibal witches. Evil stepsisters who maim their own feet to fit into a glass slipper. Eyes pecked out by watchful birds.

Heavy shit man.

So it was natural for me, at some point in my life, to do a fairy tale mashup, since these stories shaped the early days of my life as a reader. And who doesn't love a mashup?

Red Rising: The Direwolf of Murkfell combines some of my favorite fairy tales and gives them all a spin: "Beauty and the Beast", "Little Red Riding Hood", and a dash of "Snow White". And of course, a fairy tale can't be complete without witches. The Red Cloak witches (or the "Little Reds"), as forces of good, remind me of the fairies from "The Sleeping Beauty of the Wood" (after I wrote them); and Ravyn Rathmore is reminiscent of all evil fairy tales witches, but especially the evil queen from "Snow White". And Granny? Well, Granny is the coolest Granny ever to Granny.

I have worked on this story off and on for a few years, and

what began as a short story has now transformed into a novella, with the promise of even more stories to come. I hope you enjoy these new twists on old favorite fairy tale archetypes. Leaving Murkfell for other territory feels strange after so long, but I promise to return. Lucien and Thea aren't done with me—or you —yet.

I hope you will continue the journey to Moonbright with us. May the moon light your path, and happy reading!

CHAPTER 1
THE MURKFELL WOOD
THEODORA

"BEWARE THE MURKFELL, MISS MOURNINGBEAM," says the withered old man as he hands me my battered carpetbag and climbs back onto the coach to take the reins. "I'm sorry I can't take ye any further than here." He wipes the dust off his brow and fiddles with the reins, ready to leave me here, all alone in this godforsaken place.

I glance at the dark forest looming just ahead, the gnarled branches piercing the innocent blue sky that blankets me from above. I look back to the coachman, who is trying to steady the jittery horses. "I don't understand. Why can't you take me to Murkfell Village? There's a perfectly good road running through those trees that your little coach would surely navigate."

"D'ye see my horses, miss? They won't step foot into the Murkfell Wood, and you shouldn't either." The old man expertly begins to turn the coach around, his two mares following his gentle prodding.

"But where are you going? Surely you just can't leave me here in the middle of—"

"Sorry miss," he calls as he coaxes his horses up to a trot, "this is as far as I go! Beware the direwolf of the Murkfell!"

In a flourish of dust and braying of horses, I am left alone, listening to the fading pounding of the horses running away from whatever evil I am about to walk into. That horrible old man! If he knew the dangers, why did he just leave me here, all alone? Some people value gold far above a human life. But no matter. I did not need that old man or his fairy tales.

Direwolf? Surely that is just a story to scare children into not straying too far from home. Direwolves aren't real.

Taking a deep breath, I turn, pick up my satchel, and begin walking toward the darkness of the unknown wood before me. I have no choice. I have a posting in Murkfell Village as a healer and midwife, and I have to get there by tomorrow.

It's just a forest, I think, *and there is an easy path to follow straight to the village.* As I walk into the gloom of the Murkfell, my soft leather boots crunching on dead leaves, the ravens form a loose circle above me and caw, as if laughing at my foolishness for entering this place. Looking ahead of me into the wood, it is like nighttime. Behind me, the sun is still shining in a bright blue sky, the ravens outside the Murkfell are still trying to warn me from the branches of the oaks.

They do not enter with me.

That is not a good sign. But all I can do is put one foot in front of the other. Alone I trudge ahead, the branches of the trees closing in and reaching out to snag my red cloak as if to ensnare me in the living being that was the darkness of this forest. *Remember, Theodora*, I think, untangling the red wool from the clawing branches with cold, trembling fingers, *you are the light. You are a Mourningbeam. You are a Moonbright witch.*

Calling down my power, I call the light from within, as there is no light without to draw from. From my hand, a soft warm light begins to glow, and the trees shrink back, as if afraid of my light. I release the light from my hand, and it hovers before me, a luminous orb, lighting my way through the forest. I can see the eyes of owls and other creatures glowing in the dark of the twisted wood, but I fear no animal.

Humans are the real fear. Not wild animals, nor this imaginary direwolf the old coachman warned me about.

About an hour into my journey, my stomach begins to rumble, my energy flagging after the long carriage ride from Moonbright. I take shelter under a massive oak right off the path, settling into its roots and wrapping my cloak about me. I cannot believe it is daytime. I look up into the sky, mostly blotted out by the gnarled trees above, but no blue sky greets me from in between its spaces. The sky looks dark gray as if a storm is approaching. Is it always like this here?

My orb still lingers around me, comforting me with its warmth and light. I unwrap a cloth package containing a hunk of bread, cheese, and dried venison my mother had packed before I left. Homesickness tugs at my heart, weighing it down, and tears well in my eyes, but I fight the urge for self-pity. Wiping my tears and trying to look forward to my new life in Murkfell Village as a Red Cloak, I eat my modest repast nestled in the sheltering branches of the enormous oak. It feels almost as if the tree is embracing me.

I then enjoy a few sips of rich red Moonbright wine from my flask, a parting gift from my father. *"Take a nip of this to ward off the cold on your journey,"* he had said, his sapphire eyes shimmering with tears as he bade his only daughter a final goodbye. The wine warms me after a few sips and gives me the courage to continue my journey.

The cracking of twigs and dried leaves snaps me out of my reverie. It sounds as if a creature is gingerly walking about in the forest. Heart pounding, I glimpse two sets of eyes, and two deer materialize out of the shadow of the gnarly trees. My breath releases in a sigh, relieved it is only woodland creatures. Then I see more shining eyes coming toward me. Raccoons, songbirds, rabbits, squirrels, chipmunks, all emerge from the darkness of the wood and began to surround me as I sit flabbergasted, nestled in the roots of the oak. I am accustomed to animals being drawn to me, but I am surprised these creatures can even survive here.

What if they are trapped here? It is a horrible thought. This forest is not welcoming, quite the opposite. I expand the orb, spreading more warmth and light to the surrounding animals.

"You poor things," I whisper, holding up my hand as a little bluebird alights on my finger. "How do you live in such darkness and gloom?" A deer nudges my hand and I gently stroke its velvety soft head. "Follow me, little creatures, I'll lead you out of here."

I stand, gathering my belongings, and walk back onto the path, the animals still scurrying about me. I feel less frightened with the animals around me and am determined to finish my journey posthaste.

A few steps ahead, the pack of animals freezes. The chipmunks and squirrels scurry into nooks and crannies, the tiny birds alight in the gloomy trees.

I also halt, looking warily around me. *If the animals are frightened, then I should be too, right?* The deer are still as statues, their nostrils the only movement as they sniffed the stale air. Had my light also attracted the unwanted attention of a predator, like a bear or a wolf? A real wolf, not some imaginary direwolf...

I wave my hand into the orb, and it vanishes, casting me into utter darkness. Before me, two eyes glow brightly, reflecting off what, I know not. The eyes are too high to be a wolf. And human eyes do not glow. It is more than likely a bear. But the old man's voice echoes in my ear, and the thought of an enchanted beast is much worse than that of a bear.

What if is the direwolf of Murkfell?

I stand as still as possible, anxiously debating on whether to cast my light once more. But in the darkness, my fear skulks up my spine, the warnings from the old man plodding through my brain. *"Beware the direwolf of the Murkfell ..."*

Direwolves do not exist, I assure myself, taking a quiet step forward. *They went extinct thousands of years ago.*

As I take the step forward, I hear the creature move, as if it is stepping back away from me.

"I won't hurt you," I whisper into the gloom, waiting for my eyes to adjust to the darkness, but it is still pitch black, the canopy of trees consuming any light there might have been from above.

Suddenly the eyes began to move toward me. I can hear heavy paws hitting the dirt, the deer bolting back into the forest. Alone on the road, I have no choice.

I cast my light, the orb illuminating the dark road before me.

CHAPTER 2

THE DIREWOLF OF
THE MURKFELL

LUCIEN

THAT WAS CLOSE. She had almost seen me when she cast her light. But I, like the other animals in this dismal forest, am drawn to her light like a moth to flame. I had to take a closer look.

Ravyn hadn't warned me anyone was coming through the Murkfell today, much less a Red Cloak. She should have seen it in her scrying mirror. Besides being healers and midwives, the Red Cloaks are witches with elemental powers themselves, but none that rival Ravyn's. According to Ravyn. I personally have never met a Red Cloak or even seen one.

Until now.

I am walking the perimeter of the Murkfell as I usually do, when suddenly, through the gloom, I see a light glowing. Soft, warm, beckoning.

I creep toward the source of light, lest they be more hunters trying to pilfer their glory by killing the Murkfell direwolf. But I feel no malice from this light, as I have before with hunters.

From between the trees, I can finally see a young woman, dark hair cascading out of her red hood, walking purposefully yet carefully down the path toward the village. The poor soul, braving the Murkfell to get to her post in the village on time instead of going the long way around. She looks small and harmless enough to me, carrying a battered old carpetbag in one hand and a lantern in the other. But...upon closer inspection, the light is emanating from her hand, not a lantern...

Could it be?

I follow her on paws silent from Ravyn's enchantments, so I can stalk unheard. My camouflage also makes me undetectable to the human eye. But this Red Cloak is no mundane.

She is indeed a witch. And not just any witch.

I follow her for what seems like an eternity through the forest. She never feels my presence.

A witch with the power of goodness and light
can overcome Ravyn's darkness and might.

The lines from the children's poem comes unbidden to my mind, where shattered memories always lie dormant until triggered, like now. Though I had not grown up in Murkfell, I had heard the rumors as a child about a darkling witch of the wood before I made my way through the Murkfell Wood that fateful day. Then Ravyn had later told me the children's rhyme was actually a based upon a divination she had received as a young girl, from a traveling fortune teller she had escaped to late in the night.

There, in the dark tent of the diviner, the air choked with fragrant incense, a story unfolded of a formidable witch from Moonbright who would one day cause her downfall. Ravyn told me how she had boasted around the village that she would destroy any Moonbright who ever set foot into her village, her forest. The villagers scoffed, laughing at what they thought was child's play, an imaginative, orphaned little girl living inside her mind to escape the harsh realities of her life. For where else would she live?

How long have I been with Ravyn now? A decade? A century? I have no sense of time here.

. . .

BEWARE, *young child, the witch of the wood,*
   Who makes the Murk so fell;
   So wicked was she
   She had to flee
   The light of the tolling bell.

SHE BUILT *her house in the murk of the wood*
   A most unwelcoming sight
   Shields and spells
   Darkness and bells
   Her house in the Murk a true blight.

ALONE SHE LIVED, *until one morn*
   A Moonbright prince lost his way
   Sun and light
   His magic so bright
   As bright as the brightest of days.

THIS GOLDEN PRINCE, *thought the darkling witch,*
   is more powerful than I
   For the light is bright
   And drowns out my might
   He must be destroyed by and by.

FOR SHE REMEMBERED *the prophecy that haunted her so*
   Each tortuous night 'til day:
   A witch with the power of moon and light
   can overcome Ravyn's darkness and might.

. . .

So DOWN SHE called her ravens so dark
  To throng the unknowing prince
  Taken by surprise
  Even though so wise
  He was never heard from since

HER RAVENS SWOOPED, her ravens swarmed
  The prince was now her own
  With a flourish of spells
  And witch's bells
  A wolf he now is, fur to bone.

BEWARE, young child, the witch of the wood,
  Who makes the Murk so fell;
  Step not ye near
  Or Ravyn will appear
  And put ye under her spell.

IF THIS RED Cloak has the power of light, might she be the one to defeat Ravyn and banish my curse? She has to be a Moonbright witch. No other witches have the power of the cosmos, except Moonbrights. And Ravyn. But Ravyn's magick is dark, as if called from the black side of the moon or from the shadows cast by the sun itself.

I stop and sit in a dense thicket as the young woman nestles in the roots of an oak, woodland creatures encircling her, who no doubt are fascinated by her just like I am. I am a beast, after all.

Entranced, I watched her silently, barely breathing. It has been years since I have seen another human like this one. Ever since Ravyn has bound me to this beastly body, I have only been in contact with her and the arrogant hunters who want my head as some sort of gruesome trophy to prove their bravery and courage. Foolishness, more like. The other villagers are too afraid to enter here, and horses bolt before stepping foot into its black abyss. Ravyn Rathmore has made Murkfell Wood a fell wood indeed.

The animals surround the Red Cloak, entranced by the light orb that levitates above her, giving them all light and heat. Birds land on her hand, the deer licks her fingers, and the chipmunks climb into the folds of her blood-red wool cloak to curl up to nap.

Her light reminds me of... *Think no more about that. That was so long ago.*

If she is the one who can break my curse, how can I approach her without frightening her?

I watch her again through the trees as she leaves the protection of the oak. Her orb still searching curiously, the Red Cloak looks this way and that as the animals slowly emerge from the protection of the twisted trees to hover around her once more as she makes her way down the dark forest path.

She is a Moonbright witch. There was no doubt about that.

I have to figure out a way to get her to help me before I am bound to Ravyn and the Murkfell forever. And the red moon will be rising. Soon.

Very soon.

CHAPTER 3

OUT OF THE DARKNESS, INTO THE LIGHT

THEODORA

WHEN I AWAKE the next morning, I am covered in vines and night-blooming flowers that have wound themselves around me. Two does and a stag have also provided warmth and company during the cold, lonely night. Some trees almost seemed to lean over me during the night, creating a sort of shelter, while others still seem to shrink away from my presence. It is a strange mystery I haven't yet unraveled.

I gently unwind myself from the plant life, and the deer scatter as I wake and stretch, shaking off the night's broken, unsettling dreams which have settled into my stiff body like the cold.

I kept dreaming of the creature through the night, its eyes haunting my every step, but each time I cast my light there would be nothing there, exactly as it happened the night before. I know a living presence had been standing in front of me on the road, but as soon as I cast my light, there was nothing there. Even the animals had felt its presence and scurried away. They wouldn't have imagined it there as I might have. I had searched for close to an hour for the creature, never venturing too far from the path, but fatigue had forced me to end my search and take my nightly rest on the cold and unforgiving forest floor.

Although I long for the cheerful warmth of a crackling fire, I don't want to waste time on it, and it is too damp besides. I hastily eat what is left of my bread, cheese, and dried venison, take a sip of wine, and I am on my way again.

It isn't long before I begin to see tendrils of sunlight gently weaving their golden threads through the branches of the trees.

Sunlight!

I have to be close to the edge of the Murkfell. The knowledge of this quickens my pace, and the birds start twittering around me, the deer begin to frolic, and the chipmunks chitter away happily as we make our way to the light. They are as happy as I am.

My eyes squint as the light grows brighter, and I am running, my leather boots silent on the damp leaves of the forest floor. I see the border of the forest and the world of light beyond. My red cloak trails behind me, blood in the wind, my feet carrying me further away from this vile place.

The trees gradually thin out, and I explode into the light, my face upturned to the sky, reveling in the warmth of the sun. The animals rejoice alongside me, bursting in all directions, happy to be free of the forest. I can't help but laugh and give the deer a fond pat on the head before resuming my walk to the village. I can already smell the smoke from the village chimneys as it snakes its way into the sky.

I glance back at the border of the Murkwood, so dark and uninviting. Chills trace a path up my spine as I think I glimpse a glowing pair of eyes watching me through the branches.

Eyes forward, always keep your eyes forward. New future, new life. I cannot be concerned with what might be living in the Murkfell Wood. I have plenty of humans in the village to tend to. Shaking off the chill of the Murk, I turn back to the road and continue my journey.

I follow the inviting chimney smoke, curling incessantly upward to the bright blue sky. My mouth waters at the thought of a home-cooked meal after eating cheese and dried meat for the last week during my journey here. The melodious sounds of life dance in my ears: children screeching in excitement, the pleasing tinkle of women's laughter, and the booming sounds of men greeting each other as they start their day. I self-consciously begin to smooth my dirty, wrinkled dress and unbrushed hair, afraid my appearance will appall the villagers. It wasn't the best first impression, but what can I do?

Following the sounds, I come around the bend and see the first cottages, cozily tucked among the trees. The tales of the Murkfell Wood I heard before my journey certainly didn't lead me to expect such a quaint hamlet so near its borders. Sunlight pours into the center of the village, and some people mill about chatting, some are hanging the wash, the blacksmith is stoking his fire, and somewhere beyond the buildings, I hear the soft mooing of cows and the bleating of goats.

The main buildings are clustered around an open clearing, neat and tidy: the chapel, the blacksmith, the local watering hole, the mill, the bakery, and a few others I can't make out yet. It looks like any other cheery village I have visited, except for the delightful houses which span out from the village proper up into the towering trees.

While the buildings of the village are on the ground, many of the residents' cottages are built into and around the trees, built from the strong, dark wood of the Murkfell, with inviting circular porches with rounded or arched doorways. My mouth parts slightly at the wonder of such houses, such gigantic trees. I have seen nothing like it. In the distance, I can hear the rush of a river. How had I not heard that in Murkfell Wood?

It had been as silent as the grave in there.

"She's here, she's here!"

I am jerked out of my reverie by the calls of a small girl in the middle of the village, pointing toward me. Suddenly, all the villagers' heads swivel toward me. Some women drop their laundry baskets to run toward me, their faces beaming with joy, their small, dirt-smudged children in tow. Old people shuffle out of their houses, and before I know it, there is a withered man and woman, on their knees at my feet, weeping and kissing my feet and the dirtied fabric of my plain brown dress as if I were some kind of saint.

"You're here! You're really here!"

"She's going to save us all!"

"We're finally free of the witch's doom!"

"She survived the Murkfell! She is a Moonbright witch for sure!"

Hardly knowing what to say or do, I feel frozen to the spot, thankful for the appearance of another Red Cloak who appears in the throng of people.

"Please step aside! Give her space, she's only just arrived!" The Red Cloak, who seems irritated with the villagers, gives me a huge smile, takes my hand, and pulls me out of the curious multitude.

"Come this way, the Red Cloaks are down at the end of the village proper," she gestures back the way I came into the village. "We're one of the first buildings you passed on the way in. We like it quiet. I'm Amity Shadowend. And obviously, the whole village knows who you are, Theodora Mourningbeam! Are you alright?? We were so shocked when we heard you were traveling *through* the Murkfell Wood instead of around it like everyone else!" Amity looks me up and down as if to ascertain if I had any injuries. "But you are a Moonbright, so I am not surprised you made it through the Murk unscathed."

"I'm fine, just hungry and tired. Grateful to be out of the Murkwood." I push back my hood and gratefully drink in the breeze flowing through my unbound locks.

"I apologize for the villagers. We don't get many new people here, especially witches. And never a Moonbright! Your people usually never leave your kingdom, right?"

I shake my head as we pass by the smithies, the smell of coal, leather, and wood all swirling in the air as they commenced their work. "I was expecting to the subject of curiosity, just not so much."

"The apothecary is down this way, closer to the river." Amity gestures to a small building, which looks like a house. Above the door is a wooden sign with a red cloak painted upon it. "This is the apothecary, and the house next door is where we all live together. It is small, I know. There are five of us now, so you and I will have to share a room. But you won't mind, right?" Entranced by her huge smile, I couldn't help but feel welcome as pulls me into the apothecary.

Two young women swarm me as soon as I walk inside, the earthy smell of herbs and the acrid waft of smoke assaulting my nostrils. One Cloak is still sitting in a rocking chair by the fire, eyeing me suspiciously and knitting quite furiously, as if punishing the yarn.

They are all dressed alike, in simple beige wool dresses, leather lace-up boots, and brown leather corsets cinching their waists. Three red cloaks hang on a coat rack by the door.

"Theodora! We're so glad you're here!" A raven-haired beauty with night-dark skin throws her arms around me, kissing me on the cheek. "I am Elwen Riddle, earth. Amity is air—did she already tell you that? And Jemma Keeling here is water. The sourpuss over by the fire is Cordelia Bloodworth, who is our resident fire witch."

Cordelia glares at Elwen, then returns to her knitting. "Pleased to meet you," she mumbles at me, still not looking up from her work.

"It's so wonderful to meet you all!" I exclaim, surprised at my warm reception (with the exception of the fire witch). "I've not been around many elemental witches; I can't wait to learn about your magic!"

"And we yours," says Amity as she takes my muddy, dirty cloak. "We'll get this washed for you. We have a spare you can use until then." She leaves the room as Elwen pours me a cup of tea and sits me down next to the fireplace.

I sit heavily and sigh, rubbing my aching feet, wishing I could remove my boots. Elwen places a steaming mug in one hand, and a plate of warm bread, honey, and cheese in the other. "Oh, bless you! What wonderful refreshment!" I tuck gratefully into the bread and take a sip of the warming tea.

"This tea is a specialty of mine. It helps weak constitutions. You'll feel refreshed in no time!" Elwen smiles, sitting down next to me.

Jemma, the water witch, sits down on the hearth, looking a bit shy. She looks younger than the rest of us, with radiant chestnut locks, golden amber eyes, and golden skin the color of toasted acorns. She is breathtakingly beautiful. "We're so glad you're here. There are usually only four of us, one for each element. But we're stretched thin out here. We also serve Wood-borne, and there are times we cannot make it back over the mountain pass, leaving the village here shorthanded. When we received your Red Cloak application—a real live Moonbright witch—we couldn't turn you down!" Her cheeks, two shiny ripe apples, pull up into a grin. "A natural-born healer! You can heal just by touching someone, right?"

"What made you leave Moonbright to come *here* of all places?" Cordelia interrupts before I can answer, leaning against the doorjamb, glaring at me with her bright blue eyes, a stark contrast to her dark hair.

"Well, I was born with healing powers, so it was a natural calling to become a healer. I love helping people. And when I heard a local midwife mention the posting here, I thought it sounded interesting." I almost tell them about the strange pull I felt to come to this village, but I don't know them well enough to confide that. Would they think me strange? I focus once again on the conversation with my new Red Cloak sisters. "So here I am." I blow on the tea and take a dainty sip to not to burn my tongue. It tastes of clove, anise, and honey. It was blissfully warm, and a pleasant change from the wine and water I'd been drinking the last week during my travels.

"Well, whatever your reason, we're always happy to have another Red Cloak. We needed another set of hands to help us with the villagers who live deeper in the forest and up into the mountains." Amity squeezes by Cordelia and also comes to sit at the table.

"So, we must know, Thea, is it alright if I call you that?" Without waiting for an answer, the loquacious Elwen continues. "Did you see the direwolf?" Her eyes widen in excitement and suspense, and the others lean in so minutely its almost imperceptible.

I almost tell them the truth, that I had seen *something*, but I decide to keep that knowledge to myself. I don't want news of the direwolf to spark a hunting frenzy on the poor creature. "No, no wolves. Just a few woodland creatures when I got closer to the Murkfell road." I focus on drizzling more honey on my bread lest they can see the lie in my eyes.

"No one ever comes through the Murkfell Wood to get here. They take the long way 'round. Why did you brave the Murkfell when entire groups of men who are twice your size refuse to set foot in that forest?" Cordelia's eyes stab into mine.

"She's a cosmic witch, Cordelia! She has the power of light, so naturally, she can scare away all the fell creatures of the dark!" Elwen says before I could answer. She rolls her eyes. "Don't mind her. You're terribly brave, coming through the Murkfell Wood the way you did."

"The other way would have taken an extra week, and my posting started today. I had no idea the coachman would leave me like that! He said he would take me all the way to Murkfell," I said, shaking my head in disbelief.

"He did take you all the way *to* the Murkfell. Just not *through* the Murkfell. Did he ever say he would take you to Murkfell Village? There's the rub," Jemma says quietly, clearing my empty plate. "He just wants the coin, no matter how he can get it, even if means leaving someone to go through the Murkfell Wood alone."

My mouth hangs open slightly with the realization. "That horrid little man! No wonder everyone in the tavern laughed when he said he'd take me *to* the Murkfell. I did insist that I was going through the wood, and not the long way around, so I am fully to blame for this one."

Amity laughs, the corners of her mahogany eyes creasing. "Old Mr. Crowe. He's a sneaky one."

"Come on, Thea, let's get you settled in your room! Cordelia is heating water for your bath, and then you can have a rest." Elwen takes my hand and leads me over to our shared house, my new living quarters.

"Don't I need to start my work today? I'm not too tired—"

"Nonsense! Today, you rest. But tomorrow—your new life in Murkfell Village begins."

CHAPTER 4
BRING ME HER HEART
LUCIEN

"Where is she, Lucien?"

Ravyn's disembodied voice erupts in my ear. I startle and look around. She has a bad habit of disappearing for days and then suddenly reappearing.

Then beside me, her ethereal form materializes, like a thick mist. Her long, black hair undulates in the air as if she is underwater. She is projecting, her spirit floating lazily in the air in front of me, but her eyes, even in this form, are sparking with fury. Her lilac dress, or the hint of it, floats on the breeze, wisps of color in the dark forest.

Where her body is, I know not, but given the ragged appearance of her spirit, she must be out of the Murkfell.

"Who are you talking about, Ravyn?" I inquire, irritated. "And please stop showing up like that. I hate it."

"Precisely why I do it." She smirks, drifting closer. "And finding you is much easier if I project, now, isn't it?"

I back away on instinct. Ravyn is poison, corrupting everything she touches.

"I know there is a Moonbright witch here," she continues, her expression turning to a scowl. "I can still feel her presence!

Why is there a Moonbright witch in my wood? And how did she ESCAPE?"

Ravyn looms over me, growing larger by the second. But after years of her tantrums, she is no more worrisome than a cloudy day. She will never hurt me, her fierce-hearted guard of the Murk. She needs me, although she hates to admit it.

So, I can't help but taunt her. "Why weren't you here to get rid of her yourself, Ravyn Rathmore? Aren't *you* the witch of this wood?"

Her form wavers and sputters, no doubt because her anger is making her lose focus. "I can't always be here, Lucien, that's why I have you!"

"I can't be everywhere at once, despite all your impressive spell work."

"Tell me of the girl!" She spits out the words, exasperated.

I've made her edgy, irritated. If I had a human mouth, I would be smirking. Inwardly I am. I must celebrate even insignificant victories over Ravyn, or I would go mad in these prisons she has constructed around me. First the prison of this lupine body, then the prison of the Murkfell Wood.

"What was she doing in my forest?"

Ravyn's face is suddenly hovering in front of mine, her violet eyes sparking, the purple mist around her puddling around my paws.

"It appears she is a Red Cloak heading to Murkfell Village, or possibly Windborne," I confess. "She made her way through quickly enough and was gone before I knew it. I had no reason to hurt her." I lay down in the leaves, now dried and itchy on my belly without the morning dew. I begin to lick my paws casually, knowing that my casual, calm demeanor is angering Ravyn even more. I relish it.

"She obviously wasn't just any Red Cloak!" she objects. "Her Moonbright stink is all over my wood." Her eyes dart around, if the young healer would appear again any moment.

"How was I to know she was a Moonbright?" I stand and sit back on my haunches.

"Didn't she use her powers while she was here? Couldn't you feel her magick?" Ravyn demands, her spirit twitching as she floats through some branches.

Of course I felt it. "No, she walked quickly through and was on her way."

"Did she see my cottage? Or try to look for it? Or for you?" Ravyn's paranoia persists, a constant thorn in my side. "No one in the Murkfell Wood is just 'passing through,' Lucien."

"Well, as a Red Cloak she had to have been headed for Murkfell Village or Windborne, as I said before. She never deviated from the road that I saw," I clarify. "Now, if you don't mind, I need to go patrol." I stand, shaking out my fur, and turn to head south, away from the village, although I long to catch a glimpse of the young woman once more. Her beauty and light have haunted me ever since I first saw her, nestled in the roots of the oak...

"Go patrol Windborne Pass," the witch suddenly orders.

I can't believe my luck. My head snaps around at Ravyn's demand.

"From the highest point of the pass you can still see both Murkfell Village and Windborne. Watch for the Red Cloaks. The Moonbright witch should be like a beacon in the darkness wherever she goes."

Ravyn never allows me into the north woods. They were on the north side of Murkfell Village, across the river, just beyond her reach. Out of her self-claimed jurisdiction. And Granny keeps Ravyn's foul magick out of both Murkfell Village and Windborne. But this patrol means I must cross the river, pass into Granny's territory. Ravyn can't cloak her fear, even in her projection. This new witch is making her nervous if she is allowing me to willingly go beyond her borders and into Granny's.

This new patrol means I can see her again; I can find the Moonbright with the red cloak...

I take a step closer to Ravyn. "The Windborne Wood? You never allow me out of the Murk. And that's Granny's—"

"I'm fully aware of Granny's influence in the north woods," Ravyn interrupts, "but I need you to see about that witch. See if she's in Murkfell or possibly Windborne," grumbling and clenching her fists. "I can't have a Moonbright witch skulking about."

A wry laugh, which is more of a guttural growl, escapes my muzzle. "Still superstitious about the prophecy, are we?" I ask, goading her, knowing full well I too believed fully in the prophecy, as it could mean my freedom.

"Do as I say!" she bellows, once again swooping down right in front of my face, her eyes afire. "Now go! Find the witch!"

"And what shall I do when I find her?" My calm is kindling only stoking Ravyn's fiery anger further.

"Bring me her heart."

Suddenly, an ornately carved wooden box appears, tied around my neck. My heart sinks. This Moonbright was my only hope to break free of Ravyn's bonds.

"What?" I gasp. "She's an innocent girl, I won't—"

"YOU HAVE NO CHOICE!" she thunders, as the fell purple mist explodes around me and creeps into the surrounding trees. "You are my huntsman, my soldier, my assassin. You are *my* predator and the executioner of *my* will. Forever bound to *my* word."

I start at the sudden display of power. *It is a good thing her physical form isn't here.*

"Besides," Ravyn adds, gesturing towards me, "a Moonbright witch will be the most delicious prey to you, right?"

The irony of her words is cruel, but I slowly nod, playing along. *How would I get out of this one?*

RAVYN'S FORM soon fades away and I am left padding through the forest on silent paws, in my incessantly silent world. The Red Cloak once again appears in my mind, as I make my way to the Windborne Wood. I long to hear the music of her voice, like when she whispered to the woodland creatures. I need music. I need noise.

I need life.

The Murkwood is my coffin, and the rising of the red moon will be the last nail to secure it.

The one loophole in my curse is a Moonbright witch breaking the curse, nullifying it before the rising of the red moon. This phenomenon is a significant event that amplifies magick, including spells that can void others, no matter who the caster is. And the power of a Moonbright witch would be... more powerful than I could ever imagine. But if the curse is not broken before the red moon sets, I will forever be bound to Ravyn.

There will be no going back to being a human, no going back to my old life. And how I long for it, especially after seeing the young Red Cloak, so full of life, light, and love. She represented everything I have longed for since being trapped here so long ago... I cannot tell the passage of time any longer.

Ravyn had been but a young girl of about thirteen or fourteen when she entrapped me, her youth and supposed innocence allowing me to fall victim to her cunning wiles. I had gotten lost while out hunting, and she made certain she was found. She "was but an orphan" who lived in a humble shack in the woods and insisted on sharing what little food and drink she possessed with me before sending me back on my journey. Famished and exhausted, I naturally relented, hoping to secretly leave a stash of gold coins in the girl's shelter before I left. She had struck me as the type to not accept charity from anyone, even when she desperately needed it. I saw her hollow cheeks, that glint in her eye hard as diamond from a life that had already rendered her sharp enough to cut glass. I had truly wanted to help her.

And she had exploited that.

Ever since, I'd been praying for a Moonbright witch to break the curse, to defeat Ravyn so I can be free, so all the denizens of the Murkfell and its surrounding environs—all its living creatures, human and animal alike—can be free.

We are all her prisoners to a certain extent.

I have begun to despair as the years passed, and the only humans to set foot in this forest are hunters. Hunting me, the allegedly vicious direwolf of the Murkfell Wood.

I am not the vicious one. I have not killed a human since I have been trapped here.

It is all Ravyn.

As if the villagers and outlanders didn't fear her magick enough, she created her own lore about her ferocious direwolf guard of the Murkfell over the years. She would rip apart bodies with expert care, leaving entrails scattered just outside the Murkwood, so the villagers could see "my" ferocity.

But I am no killer.

I just need help. I need to be set free.

And the Red Cloak is my only hope.

CHAPTER 5

THE WARDS OF WINDBORNE

THEODORA

THE NEXT MORNING, I awaken late, the sun streaming through the curtains to fall gently upon my face. I smile, excited for my new life here in Murkfell. The villagers are kind, and my Red Cloak sisters have already made me feel at home here.

I dress in my new uniform, the same beige woolen dress and leather corset that my sisters wore the day before and go downstairs.

Elwen and Cordelia are in the kitchen, a plate of bread, boar, cheese, and apples awaiting me. My mouth waters.

"Thea! You're up!" Elwin enthusiastically pipes up. "We saved you some breakfast!" She leads me to the table where I immediately dive into the delectable food.

"It's nearly time for luncheon," Cordelia intones lifelessly, giving me a side-eye from the counter where she is chopping herbs.

"I apologize for sleeping so late," I say sheepishly, then inquire after Jemma and Amity's whereabouts in between crunches of apple.

Cordelia stops her chopping and searches in her apron pockets. "They are out with patients, and I have a list for you" she answers, still searching. "Elwen and I are preparing new

medicines and potions today. We need help gathering materials."
She thrusts a piece of paper in my hand with different herbs,
plants, and flowers listed on it. "You can find these all in the
Windborne Wood, just across the bridge. Don't go into the
Murkfell again. It's too dangerous."

"Okay...but I was fine before," I object. "I don't mind
going—"

"Thea, we can't let you go into the Murk again," Elwin interrupts, "even if you were safe before. Rumor has it that Ravyn
Rathmore wasn't in the Murkfell the other day, or you would
have fallen into some trouble for sure. None of us go there,
ever. Nothing really grows there anyway, save for some mushrooms. Stay in the Windborne Wood. It's protected by Granny's
wards, so Ravyn and her fell beast can't get to you." She
squeezes my hand and smiles, picking up a basket of freshly
picked herbs for distillation and taking them to the potions
room.

"Granny? Who is Granny?" I ask, my meal finished. I stand
to wash them, but Cordelia quickly takes the crockery out of my
hands.

"I'll take these. You better get going." Cordelia's blade-sharp
eyes gesture to the basket on the table. "Granny lives in the
north woods, up the Windborne Pass. She's protected us from
Ravyn for as long as I can remember. That's why you're safe in
her Wood."

Putting on my cloak and grabbing my basket, I meet Elwen
outside and we walk beyond the chapel toward the river, which
flows through the forest.

I gasp.

Beyond the bank of the river is a wall of wards, extending up
through the trees from the river. I can't see where they end. The
glimmering white sigils dance their way from the forest floor up
to the sky.

"This is ancient magick," I whisper, in awe of the sight. "I've
never even seen wards this impressive, even in Moonbright!" I

exclaim, wondering at Granny's handiwork. "And I can pass through these?"

"As long as you aren't Ravyn Rathmore, you can pass through these just fine," Elwin replies. "Do you have your list?" As I nod my consent, she continues her instructions. "Keep the village in sight so you don't get lost. You won't have to go far to find these."

I nodded, understanding my task.

"Good. Well, if you don't have any questions, then I'll see you soon!" Elwen chirps, heading back to the apothecary with a smile and a wave.

I take a deep breath and cross the short wooden bridge over into the Windborne Wood with no issues from Granny's wards, even though I keep expecting to walk into a barrier of some sort. I look up again at the shimmering wards. The intricate sigils are the handiwork of a talented witch indeed. I can't wait to meet this mysterious Granny.

I begin foraging, the items easy enough to find: dandelion, elderberry, hawthorn, burdock, black cohosh, mushrooms.

I enjoy the cool, crisp, early fall breeze, the sunshine on my skin, the birds chatting away in the trees. It is easy to forget the gloom of the Murkfell Wood here, and my spirit feels lighter than air in this beautiful place with each passing moment. The trees soar into the sky, creating a ceiling of evergreen above me. I pick a few fragrant needles for good measure; they will make a lovely tea. The sound of the birds and the river are the only sounds I can hear. I feel as if I am in a cathedral. I spot some lovely mushrooms growing some distance off the path, and wander in the area foraging, my promise to keep the village in sight quickly forgotten under the spell of the lush greenery and sharp, evergreen air.

I am kneeling on the ground, gingerly placing fresh mushrooms in my basket when I hear footfalls through the wood, twigs snapping, leaves crunching underfoot. Maybe Elwen or Cordelia have come to join me. I look around and realize I can no longer see the chapel or treehouses from the village. I had wandered too far.

I follow the sound of the footsteps, looking down as I walk to not trip over the immense tree roots crisscrossing the forest floor.

"Elwen is that—"

The words freeze in my mouth. My entire body goes still, except for my heart, which is pounding furiously in my chest, threatening to burst.

The direwolf of Murkfell is standing right in front of me. I know because it is far too large to be a normal wolf.

The beast is enormous, but terrifyingly beautiful, its thick fur tan and marbled with white and gray, its amber eyes burning into mine. He is taller than I am, but he is on all fours.

How did he get past Granny's wards? The basket of herbs slips from my hand, forgotten, as I begin to back up slowly.

What do I do? My breath hitches, the panic taking hold, constricting my chest. I take a deep breath, trying to steady myself. I have no idea if my magick will work on this creature, or within Granny's wards. I don't want to wait around to find out.

So, I run. My legs feel like jelly, threatening to collapse under my weight as I jump over tree roots and maneuver around brambles that keep snagging my cloak.

The beast is behind me, crashing through the forest, in pursuit. I can finally see the river up ahead, Granny's wards showing me the way back to the village.

Suddenly my cloak snags again, violently knocking me on my back, nearly taking my breath. The direwolf stands over me, slavering, its golden eyes alight with the thought of a fresh kill. I close my eyes and think of my parents, my village, my clan, all in a flash that is also an eternity. I hear a low growl emitting from its throat, so deep and close I can feel it reverberating through my entire chest. It slowly walks around to stand over me, its glowing gaze boring into mine.

There is something about the beast's eyes. They seem so... human.

He lowers his muzzle closer to my face, and I hold my breath, closing my eyes tightly. I call down my magick, as I have no choice. I feel it coursing through my body, tingling in my hands. I slowly lift my palms, ready to let loose a blast of blinding light, enough to allow me to escape.

But before I can, it speaks. *He* speaks.

"Help me," he whispers, human words emitting from his lupine mouth.

My eyes widen, incredulous. The beast is speaking. To *me*. He doesn't want to eat me.

I open my mouth to speak, but I hear my name echoing through the forest.

"Theodora!" Cordelia's voice rings through the silent wood.

"Thea! Where are you?" Then Elwen's melodic voice now joins Cordelia's, almost like two birds singing.

I must have been gone too long, and now Elwen and Cordelia are searching for me.

The beast's head jerks up, looking toward the village and back at me, his sunlit eyes pleading.

Then he leaps, running through the forest on silent paws, leaving me shocked and alone, waiting for my sisters to find me.

CHAPTER 6
THE WITCH OF WINDBORNE
LUCIEN

HER MOON-GRAY EYES still consume me, swallowing me whole.

The way she had looked at me before I even spoke...it was like she knew I wasn't truly a beast. Had she sensed the human trapped within the beast before the words left my mouth?

If her sisters hadn't come along, I might have been able to calm her, speak to her, tell her my problem, plead for her help.

But when I heard the women calling her name through the trees, I bolted. I couldn't take any chances. Now the villagers would know that I had been in the Windborne Wood, despite Granny's wards, and they would begin the hunt. Unless she didn't tell. But why *wouldn't* she?

Feeling restless, I run up the pass to an overlook with a view of the village. From there I can see three Red Cloaks clustered around her.

Theodora. Her name is like a whisper itself, and I long to call to her again. My mind, like my heart, is racing. I am also concerned. Had I hurt her? If so, I certainly hadn't mean to. I make a mental note to check later.

Suddenly a dead rabbit thumps at my feet, arresting my attention.

"Fresh kill."

Granny. I turn around, and before me stands a wizened old woman, her long gray hair interwoven with wildflowers. Her kind blue eyes, the same cerulean as her embroidered robes, sparkle and crinkle at the corners.

"Hello, Granny. I trust you are doing well," I greet, then thank her for the rabbit before sitting on my haunches to tear through the flesh of the plump little creature. Despite the human still lurking within me, I have quite the taste for raw meat now.

"You're welcome, Lucien," she kindly replies, ruffling the fur on my head. "What trouble are you brewing in my wood, young man? Why did Ravyn let you out of the Murk?" She sits next to me on a stump, taking flowers out of her basket and weaving them together.

"She wants me to kill the new Red Cloak," I answer in between bites, licking my jowls.

"Why is that? She's never bothered with them before." Granny's gnarled, arthritic fingers work surprisingly fast, weaving the flowers into a crown.

"She came through the Murkfell Wood on the way to the village, unlike everyone else who takes the long way around."

Granny's face lifts, clearly impressed with the young woman. "Very brave of her," she acknowledges. "How did she survive, then? Doesn't Ravyn kill everyone who enters her wood and then blame it on you?"

I sigh softly. "Usually, yes, but she was out of the wood that day. I have not the slightest idea where she went, though."

"It's probably best you don't know," Granny adds, then notices the box tied around my neck and asks about it. She then pokes it with her finger, the knuckle swollen. Her fingers resemble the twisted branches of the Murkfell Wood.

"It's for the poor girl's heart."

Granny shakes her head, tsking. "That Ravyn! Killing an

innocent girl! And for what? Walking through her wood to get to her post on time?"

"It's not that, Granny, she...she's..." I hesitate, not knowing if she will believe me. But it's Granny, my only friend in this world. Of course she'll believe me.

"Yes, yes, spit it out, boy!"

I hold Granny's gaze. "She's a Moonbright witch."

A sudden hush befalls us both for a brief moment.

"A Moonbright, you say?" Granny gasps. "They usually don't leave their kingdom, you know," she says softly, contemplating me meaningfully. "Ravyn wants the Moonbright's heart in a box to protect her from the prophecy." It's a statement, not a question. Granny knows Ravyn all too well.

"Yes, Granny, that's the gist of it," I confess, before gazing back down at the village. The Red Cloaks are now gone, the villagers milling about.

"Stupid girl!" Granny scolds. "Doesn't she know there is no getting around a prophecy?" She stands, her knees creaking as she does so. "Come, boy, let's go find a heart for your darkling witch."

🐾

IT TAKES A COUPLE OF HOURS, but Granny and I find a boar, which I quickly dispatch. I drag it back to Granny's cottage, high up in the Windborne mountains, where she cuts out the boar's heart and disappears with it for a time, "to work her magic in peace," as she always says. I never argue with Granny. She has strange, powerful, ancient magic, but I have never seen her practice it before; she prefers to be alone.

A while later, Granny comes back with the heart wrapped in black velvet cloth, which she carefully places in the box, then ties it back around my neck.

"Now, go take that to your darkling witch," she instructs

gruffly. "She'll leave the Moonbright girl alone, at least for a while. And then we can get to work."

I cock my head, curious. "Work? What work?"

She grins. "Getting the little moon witch to break your curse, of course."

CHAPTER 7

THE PRINCE AND THE WOLF

THEODORA

I BREATHLESSLY RUN toward Elwen and Cordelia's voices, finally catching up to them near the river. The panic ceases, the energy leaves my body in a rush, and I suddenly sink to my knees.

"Thea!" Elwen exclaims, running over and putting her arms around my shoulders to help me off the ground. "What happened?" Concern rings her eyes as she leads me back over the little bridge back into the village, beyond the reach of Granny's shining sigils.

I gasp, "I saw—"

Help me. His voice suddenly echoes through my head.

"I saw a b-bear, that's all," I stammer, before stopping to catch my breath and calm my fluttering heart.

The beast's eyes still haunt me. Glowing amber orbs, pleading. So human that I couldn't have the villagers hunting this poor creature. He spoke to me. So, there is still a human inside, waiting to be set free. An enchantment, no doubt. I *had* to help.

Cordelia sighs. I can feel her eyes roll without even seeing her. "I see you dropped your basket," she points out, sighing. "I'll go back and fetch it."

"I can go, Cordelia!" I offer, untangling myself from Elwen's protective grasp and following Cordelia back over the bridge.

"No, you've already caused enough trouble, putting us behind schedule," she objects. "Go with Elwen." She dismisses me in a huff and stomps off into the woods.

Elwen smiles and beckons me to follow her. "Come on, Thea, you can help me make potions," she says, putting her arm around me as I join her.

As we walk into the village, Amity and Jemma rush over.

"Thea!" Amity calls out, breathless. "What happened? We heard there was a ruckus in the wood." Her face is laced with concern.

"Did you get lost?" Jemma asks. "I got lost my first time in the Windborne Wood too!"

"Well," I begin sheepishly, "I did wander too far despite Elwen's warnings. Then I saw a bear, that's all. I didn't mean to alarm anyone."

"Best not stray too far in these woods," Amity advises. "Many predators afoot! I'm so glad you're alright though! A bear! How frightened you must have been." She gathers her basket with a wave and heads off to continue her work.

"Let's go make some tinctures and potions, Theodora," Elwen says, pulling me along to the apothecary.

I stop her when I spot a puppet master outside his workshop with his marionettes, giving an impromptu performance to a small group of giggling children. "I want to see this, if that is alright," I tell Elwen, already gravitating towards the show with a smile on my face, entranced. One of the marionettes is of a young girl with long, flowing black hair, and was wearing a violet dress, while the other was of a man with golden skin and amber eyes. A quiver of arrows is slung across his back, as he wields a bow in his hand. A simple crown with a small moon on it sits upon his head. The craftsmanship is exquisite. The crown is an exact replica of a Moonbright crown.

"...*alone she lived, until one morn, a Moonbright prince lost his way,*" the puppet master narrates, dangling the hunter marionette in his sun worn, wrinkled hand. The golden crest of Moonbright sits upon the marionette's chest. *"Sun and light, his magic so bright, as bright as the brightest of days...so down she called her ravens so dark to swarm the unknowing prince!"* Ravens suddenly swarm the poor, hapless prince. *"Taken by surprise, even though so wise, he was never heard from since..."*

Now the prince is replaced by a wolf, but the puppet master stops and looked at me. "I'm just rehearsing, miss, so this isn't the tale entire..." he clarifies. "Are you familiar with the poem of how the Murkwood direwolf came to be?" The old man's eyes twinkle in the sunlight.

All the children turn and look up at me, then realizing who I am, scramble to crowd around me, clutching at my cloak. I smile, patting their heads, then look back at the puppeteer.

"No, I've never heard this tale, but do keep going," I urge, wishing for him to finish. The male puppet also has amber eyes... just like the wolf I'd met in the wood. I have lived in Moonbright my entire life but have never heard that one of our princes had been enchanted and turned into a wolf. When I was younger, I remember tales of a handsome young prince who had gone on a hunting trip and had fallen from his stallion, later succumbing to his injuries.

Was that old fairy tale the real tale of the prince who is trapped inside the wolf? I wonder.

Had the Moonbright monarchy lied to cover up the truth?

"You'll see the entire performance at the Red Moon Festival, miss," the puppet master tells me, "but I'm happy to perform it for you now if you wish." He tilts his head as if granting me a wish.

"We really must go, Thea." Jemma suddenly takes my arm and begins to gently lead me away. She turns and waves at the old man. "Goodbye, Ezekiel! We can't wait for your performance!"

"He is very talented. Does he make those puppets?" I ask as we head to the apothecary.

"Oh yes, he makes all sorts of wonderful toys for the children," she replies. "You'd never know by his looks now, but he used to be a woodsman. He would take the scrap wood and make toys for his own children, then he kept up the practice even after his children were grown. Now that he's too old to cut down trees, he's content with just making toys from the scraps the young woodsmen bring him. But the puppets are his favorite."

I nod, my mind racing, images of princes, wolves, and witches flooding through my mind.

We walk into the apothecary, hanging our cloaks beside the door, and go to the potions room, where Elwen is already busy with her work.

"Is that true what he said about the direwolf?" I wonder aloud, taking a mortar and pestle and grinding a handful of herbs. "Was he a Moonbright prince before he was enchanted?"

Jemma nods, then clarifies. "Well, it's the story *we've* always been told, at least. We cannot truly know if a prince is trapped inside the wolf. But the creature is one of Ravyn's creations, of that we have no doubt."

I keep grinding, my mind working just as furiously as my hands. "So, what happens in the poem? After the prince is turned into the wolf?"

Elwin looks up, raising her eyebrows. "You've never read the poem or heard the lore of the Murkwood direwolf before?" she inquires, walking over to some sprouting herbs planted in a pot. "He was a Moonbright prince, after all. Well, *allegedly*." She then waves her hands over the plants, where they suddenly grow to full size.

My eyes widen in amazement, just as Cordelia comes in and stokes the fire by simply waving her hands in front of it.

"I have to say, your elemental magick is quite something!" I exclaim, fingering the herbs to make sure they were actually real. "Very handy. Anyway," I turn back to my work and the previous conversation, "in Moonbright we were told the prince died due to a fall from his horse while out hunting. That's it. No evil witches or curses. Just a simple, albeit tragic, accident."

Jemma bites her lip, looks at me, then fills jars with water—

with her magick, not by fetching water from the water pump in the kitchen. "Well, according to the lore, the prophecy says the only person who can save him is a Moonbright witch. And here you are, out of nowhere, when we've never had a Moonbright witch come to Murkfell Village."

Cordelia scoffs, rolling her eyes. "Jemma, you silly girl. She is but one Moonbright witch from a clan of hundreds."

My mind swirls. Something is amiss here. A Moonbright prince was lost during a Murkfell Wood hunting excursion a decade ago, and now there is a direwolf stalking the same wood. A direwolf who can also speak and comprehend language. Its words echo in my mind once more—

Help me.

It tears at my heart. I then decide that I am going to find this wolf again to do my own investigation.

Even if it means going back to the Murkfell Wood.

CHAPTER 8

HER VENOMOUS PRESENCE

LUCIEN

WITH THE ENCHANTED boar's heart in tow, I make my way back to Ravyn's cottage in the Murkfell. Leaving the protection of the Windborne Wood and reentering the Murkfell Wood hits me like a brick wall. In Granny's wood, my mind at least feels free, even if my body is still trapped within this beast. I can do what I want there without fear of Ravyn's eye always watching, her wrath lying in wait like a poisonous snake. It is a feeling I am rarely allowed.

The darkness instantly closes in around me, and I feel suffocated like never before.

I show my pace, hesitating. If I return the heart now, I won't be able to come and go into the Windborne Wood. It would be harder to see Granny and Theodora. And wouldn't Ravyn be suspicious if I turned up with the heart so soon?

I stop in my tracks and turn around, heading back into Windborne to bury the box in a safe place. With Granny's enchantments, it wouldn't rot. It would look fresh whenever Ravyn did open it.

Not wanting to go all the way up the mountain to Granny's, I bury it at the Windborne Pass overlook beneath a fragrant conifer. I look down at the village in the hopes of glimpsing Theodora, but I see no Red Cloaks milling about.

I then trudge back to the Murkfell Wood.

Back to Ravyn.

I turn off the main forest road and head west, deeper into the Murk. The closer I get to Ravyn's cottage, the more I can see and feel her dark power. The Murkwood dryads, also under Ravyn's influence, materialize out of the trees, watching me silently as I walk past. The trees here are all dead and leafless, even blacker, even more twisted than the ones on the main road. The dryads' glowing eyes seem to float, two pinpricks of light, here and there, deeper within the wood.

The fell purple mist Ravyn uses as a security measure snakes around my paws. I am getting closer. If I were human, the poisonous mist would have killed me by now.

As the mist grows thicker, I finally spy Ravyn's cottage, hewn from the blackest trees she could find, hulking silently amidst the trees. It is a sight better than the hovel she was living in when I got lost in her wood. This is no welcoming cottage, like Granny's or the ones in Murkfell Village. She has cursed and poisoned everything around her. The dead trees and their corrupted dryads stand like sentinels around her cottage, protecting her.

Ravyn is outside, standing over her immense cauldron, the contents within bubbling profusely.

She doesn't look up as I come into her boundary. Instead, she keeps stirring the pot. "What news, wolf?" she asks, leaning down and picking up two crow's feet and tossing them into the mixture. It hisses and pops for a few seconds, then dies back down.

"I haven't located her in Murkfell Village yet. I'll need a few more days to see if she's in Windborne village." My eyes catch her gaze and don't let go. If I believe the lie, then so will she.

She looks up then, her strange violet eyes glaring at me. "Where's the box?" she demands, pointing to my neck.

Movement in the corner of my eye catches my attention. The dryads are slowly making their way closer to me. Despite being Ravyn's creature, the dryads still do not trust me. They sense my disdain for Ravyn. I haven't submitted to her completely, the way they did. "I buried it for safekeeping. It was cumbersome. Do not worry, I'll use the box when the time comes."

"Then go, and do not come back until you have her heart in that box. Before the red moon rises," she adds, as if I'd forgotten the red moon and all its significance.

My heart leaps at her orders, but I stifle the burgeoning joy so Ravyn can't sense it. "Of course. It is my directive. I will not fail you," I promise as I turn to walk away from her venomous presence.

"And Lucien?" she calls before I'm out of earshot, "I'll know if that heart is bewitched in any way that is designed to trick me. I'll be able to sense the Moonbright magick, even if her heart is no longer beating."

I gulp. Would she sense Granny's enchantments? She said her magick was undetectable, even by Ravyn. But I can't take any chances.

I have to talk to Granny and devise a new plan.

I have to save Theodora, so she can save me.

CHAPTER 9

THE PLAN

LUCIEN

"What is the plan, Granny?"

Granny and I are trekking up to her cottage, higher up on the mountain. Granny, despite her age, climbs the steep hill with no sign of fatigue or shortness of breath. Despite her wizened appearance, she is as hale as one of the youngsters from Murkfell Village.

"You spoke to her, yes?" She looks back at me, and I nod my assent. "That was the first step. She knows you are not trying to eat her for breakfast now. That is good."

Granny's tiny cottage comes into view, tucked between the firs and conifers. Ivy climbs up the walls, moss covers the roof, and ferns grow in abundance all around the little house. Smoke curls out of the chimney, escaping into the infinite sky above. It was so quiet and peaceful, so unlike Ravyn's fell cottage in the Murk.

She disappears inside and begins preparing tea, leaving the door open for me. I sit in the doorway, as I am too large to fit inside her tiny kitchen without making a horrible mess.

"About the boar's heart, Granny. Ravyn says she'll know if it's not a real Moonbright heart. She says she can sense the magic. I can't kill her, Granny, I can't!" I exclaim, shaking my massive head.

Granny scoffs, turning from the stove to shake her knobby finger at me. "First thing's first—we have to set it up so the girl can meet you properly. It all begins there."

"What do you have in mind?"

"I plan to set a trap for her." She plops some leaves in a cup while she waits for her water to boil.

"A trap? What do you mean, a trap? I don't want to hurt her, Granny!"

"Nor do I, you impetuous thing. Now, close your muzzle and listen."

While Granny drinks her tea, she tells me she knows of a small sinkhole not far from where the Red Cloak had been foraging earlier, near a large patch of black cohosh. Granny would cover it with branches and leaves, the girl would fall in, and I would save her, thus making her grateful to me and more apt to listen to my pleas for help.

"How deep is this sinkhole? Won't she get hurt when she falls into it? Can't you write her a letter telling her of my plight instead?"

Granny smiles and scratches behind my ears. My back leg begins to thump on the ground, and Granny giggles. She never tires of this.

"So like a pet you are, I don't know why these fool villagers are even afraid of you."

"That's Ravyn's doing. And my size doesn't help." I paw gently at Granny's hand to keep scratching behind my ears.

She laughs and keeps scratching. "Do not worry, child, the sinkhole is not too deep, but deep enough where she can't climb out without help. We will line it with plenty of leaves and needles to break her fall. And if she's a Moonbright witch as you say, she can heal herself even if she does get hurt, yes? As for the letter...do you think she would come alone into a strange wood to meet a mysterious person? I think not."

I sigh. I am not sure of this sinkhole idea, but I really cannot think of any other options. The girl ran the last time I approached her, so I am going to have to make her my captive audience like Granny is suggesting.

"I'll be nearby. I will cast a spell so the villagers won't hear anything."

There seems to be no end to Granny's mysterious magick. Most witches have one talent, like the elemental witches who serve in the village, but Granny's magick seems to have no bounds. But even she couldn't break Ravyn's enchantment; it has to be a Moonbright witch to undo the spell.

"After you talk with her, tell her what you need, then we'll figure out our next step. But first, we must have the young witch in our corner." Granny produces a piece of dried venison from her pocket and offers it to me. I take it gently from her hand.

Why can't everyone be as kind to me as Granny?

After our modest repast, Granny and I wind our way down the pass back to the wood and spend the afternoon setting the trap for the Red Cloak. *Theodora*. Her name is like birdsong in my ears. I make sure Granny puts a thick layer of leaves on the bottom to break her fall.

"Tomorrow morning, the Red Cloak will come again to forage. And then you can plead your case." Granny pats my head as we look upon our handiwork.

"How are you so certain it will be her to come foraging? Or that she'll come in this direction again?" I look toward the village, where I can smell the smoke from the chimneys and hear the ping of the blacksmith's hammer, but I cannot see the village, which was a good sign. That hopefully means they would not see me either.

"Oh, don't worry about that, my darling boy. Old Granny will take care of everything."

CHAPTER 10

THE TRAP

THEODORA

THE NEXT MORNING, I awake to the gentle pattering of rain. The house sounds quiet. I rise reluctantly, wishing I could spend the morning lying in bed reading while it rains. But alas, duty calls.

Downstairs, Cordelia is upending everything in sight in the kitchen and potions room. "What happened to all the black cohosh I picked yesterday? It's all gone!" She throws down a wooden bowl angrily, stomping back into the potions room. I follow her.

"Can I help?" I ask, tentatively. Cordelia is intimidating at her best; in a foul mood, she's downright frightening.

She whirls around, her blue eyes blazing against the red of her hair. "Moon witch! What have you done with all the baskets of black cohosh? Mrs. Huddleston needs it for her hot spells and nerves, and the longer she goes without it, the crabbier she gets. We had baskets full in the storage house yesterday!"

"I have not seen them, Cordelia."

She narrows her eyes and stalks past me. "Well, you're the one who is going out in the rain to fetch some more. Everyone else is too busy."

"That is fine, Cordelia, I'll be happy to. I just need to eat first."

She sighs and returns to her work in the potions room while I eat a quick repast, down a cup of tea, and don my red cloak to enter the Windborne Forest again. Where had the cohosh disappeared to? Surely the other girls wouldn't have taken it from the storage house.

The gentle rain persists as I wend my way across the bridge into Windborne. Granny's sigils shimmer all around me, above me, and possibly even below me. These are powerful wards, there is no doubt. But how had Ravyn's direwolf gotten past them? Animals can easily pass through wards, as they were pure of heart and spirit.

But an enchanted beast is another story altogether.

I thought I had seen some cohosh closer to the village the day before, but now there is none to be found. I veer off the path, eyes searching for the plant. But every few seconds, my eyes keep scanning the wood for signs of the wolf.

I spy some cohosh and pick my way through the wet and slippery tree roots to get to it. As careful as I am trying to be, I still trip and fall. But instead of landing on solid ground, I find myself falling instead.

With a small yelp, I thud harshly on the ground, though it is full of leaves and needles. My shoulder throbs as I sit up, rubbing it. I try to move it, but it feels dislocated.

Thank the gods I am a natural-born healer.

I close my eyes, sitting quietly, and allow my body to begin to heal itself. The warmth pulses through me, and the celestial light within me brightens the dark, wet hole I now find myself in. I grimace slightly as my shoulder mends, then take a deep breath. I look myself over and stand to make sure I have no more injuries. Besides scrapes and bruises, I am fine otherwise.

About to scream for help, a long thick vine thumps its way down into the hole and nearly hits me in the head. I look up but can see no one. When I tug on the vine, it holds strong.

"Thank you!" I call up to my invisible rescuer, scrambling for a foothold, but I am lifted out of the hole before I take two steps.

I scramble over the edge and crawl onto solid ground, far from the sinkhole, and flop on my back, panting.

And beside me is the direwolf, with the vine in its mouth.

With another startled cry, I instinctively scoot back, trying to find purchase to stand.

The vine falls out of his mouth and lands at his feet.

Without thinking, I bolt.

The damp earth sinks beneath my feet, slowing my run. I toss my basket, pulling up my skirts and cloak in one hand to keep from tripping. My heart is in my throat. I draw breath, but don't feel it.

Am I breathing?

I risk a look back, and the wolf is giving chase, his footfalls making no sound on the loamy forest floor. With his size and weight, I should be able to hear him, but I can't.

I make a quick right, trying to get closer to the village for help, but my cloak snags and I am yanked violently backwards, landing on my back with a thud. Then the wolf is dragging me across the muddy ground, me kicking and screaming, but no one is coming to my aid.

It's as if my screams are being silenced.

I try to slip out of my cloak, but it is tangled around me. He is dragging me by the hood. As my fingers attempt to undo the latch, I do not see where the wolf if taking me.

With an unceremonious toss, I am back in the same hole I had just escaped from.

I sit up, rubbing my head. It is throbbing.

"Please do not be frightened. I won't hurt you." A gentle and melodic voice weaves in and out of the rain, drifting down to me.

"I am sorry I ran. You're the wolf that I saw the before, the d-direwolf. W-who are you?" I stammer, slowly standing up and brushing the dirt off my cloak.

"I am Lucien. I am so sorry I frightened you again. I would never hurt you. Or anyone for that matter." His amber eyes hold mine, so sincere, pleading with me to believe him.

"My name is Theodora. I'm a Red Cloak in Murkfell." I mirror my voice to his, soft, treading lightly.

A vine uncoils itself down into the hole like before, and with the assistance of the wolf, I am back on solid ground.

"I know. I saw you when you traveled through the wood to get to the village." Lucien takes a step closer, but this time I don't back away.

"That *was* you. I knew I saw something on the road, but when I cast my light, you were gone." Despite already being soaked through and beginning to shiver, I pull my hood further forward over my face as the rain grows heavier, as if it will help.

"My lady, may I please speak with you on a very important matter? I believe you're the only one who can help me." He steps closer still.

We inch closer and closer to one another; our eyes lock the entire time.

"You asked me to help you yesterday. What do you need? I will try to help you if I can."

Another step closer, his eyes burning gold. "It will take a long time to explain."

Another. I can feel his warm breath on my skin.

"I cannot tarry," I explain, cursing myself for leaving the basket in the hole. Cordelia was going to have my head on a spike in the village square.

"Tomorrow? At Granny's?" There was an urgency yet excitement to his speech, and the excitement spreads to me. "I will tell her to request you to come to see her. She can say she is ailing."

I nod, glancing back toward the village. "Of course. I hate to leave, but I better go...the Cloaks are waiting for me." Without breaking eye contact, I back away, now feeling the anxiety of showing up late without a basket.

"Of course. Until the morrow, then." Even though a beast, his manners are oddly human. He inclines his head as a goodbye and lopes up the mountain pass toward Windborne village.

I finish gathering the plants, using my skirt as a basket, and head back to the village to count the minutes until I can again meet the wolf.

No, not the wolf.

Lucien.

CHAPTER 11

ALL THAT'S GOOD
AND BRIGHT

LUCIEN

THE SKY THREATENS RAIN. Maybe she wouldn't come.

"Stop pacing, boy, you're making me nervous." Granny peers over her shoulder to glare at me, then returns to whatever is bubbling in her cauldron.

"I'm sorry, Granny, I can't help it. I am so afraid she won't show up."

"Then go down to the overlook to watch for her and get out of my hair," Granny orders, pointing her crooked finger at me to go. "I have a meal to finish preparing."

Glad to have a purpose, I run down the pass, enjoying the physical exertion. I had been sitting at Granny's most of the day. At least here in Granny's territory, I can have true peace, without worrying about Ravyn (or her spirit) materializing when I least expect it.

I sit down on my haunches on the rocky overlook, which has an unobstructed view of the village. I can see a red hooded cloak, violently crimson against the green of the forest, bobbing through the trees, making its way to the pass.

It is her.

I run down to meet her and escort her to Granny's. Her beauty grasps at my heart. No princess has ever looked so lovely, despite her plain dress, muddy at the hem. Pale skin, cheeks flushed from the cold autumn wind coming down the mountain pass, her long dark hair a braided rope hanging over her shoulder, red cloak flowing behind her. In her delicate hands she grasps a covered basket, no doubt containing a variety of remedies for Granny, to keep up the ruse.

We do not speak much, but she keeps shyly glancing my way as I lope along beside her, her clear gray eyes clutching at mine. She is still cautious, I can feel that, but her curiosity seems to outweigh any fears she might have been harboring.

"Thank you for coming," I say softly, breaking the silence as we walk off the path into the woods to Granny's cottage.

"I wouldn't have been able to stay away," she answers, giving me a small smile with rosy, pink lips. A strand of hair escapes her braid and blows across her face. How I wish I had hands to tuck it back in place. "I hardly slept last night."

Granny comes walking out of the cottage to greet us. "Well, I finally get to meet the new Red Cloak Murkfell has been chattering about! Come in out of the cold, child. I've made soup and tea, and the bread is almost ready."

"Thank you so much, that sounds delightful. May I call you Granny?" Theodora asks as she takes off her cloak and hangs it by the door.

"Of course, my girl, everyone does," Granny smiles kindly as she closes the bottom of the door, leaving the top open so I can lean in and talk with her. "As you can see, Lucien here is too large to fit in my tiny cottage, so I must keep the door open. Come sit next to the fire so you won't catch a chill, Theodora." Granny beckons Theodora over and nestles her by the fire, handing her a cup of tea.

"You know my name?" she asks, wrapping her hands around the mug and inhaling the aroma before taking a sip.

"Of course, I do, Lucien told me. Lucien, why don't you tell the poor girl why she's here?" Granny ladles soup into two wooden bowls and tosses an uncooked, skinned rabbit my way. "And don't talk with your mouth full."

Theodora smiles at that, her eyes sparkling, brighter than the crackling fire beside her.

I take a deep breath and dive into my entire story, prefacing it with the prophecy Ravyn had received as a child from a diviner. My story wended its way to the day I wandered alone into the Murkfell Wood after escaping my hunting party, explaining the curse, and the significance of the red moon.

"Well, Theodora, I need your help, as you know. The red moon is rising, and it is rising soon. I am not sure how long it has been, but Granny believes it has been at least ten years since Ravyn enthralled me. There is only one person who can break the spell; and that is you."

Theodora places her bowl on the table and walks over to the door. She gazes deeply into my eyes. "So the children's poem is actually true? Only a Moonbright witch can save you?"

"Yes," I answer quickly, returning her equally intense gaze. "Only a Moonbright witch can break the spell. But it must be before the rising of the red moon, or I am trapped in this wolf body, forever bound to Ravyn."

Concern laces her eyes as she turns back to Granny. "What is the red moon, Granny?"

"It is the apex of all magic that comes only once a century. Any curse can be broken, with the right knowledge, no matter who the hexer is. Even one as strong as Ravyn," Granny says between mouthfuls of rich broth.

"Then why can't you break the spell?" Theodora wonders aloud.

"Because only a Moonbright witch has the power to undo her enchantment. I am no Moonbright. You are, however. And your power is the polar opposite of Ravyn's. She is the last of the Sundark clan." Granny walks over to stand in front of Theodora, taking her by the upper arms. "And you have very strong lunar magick. Am I correct, girl?"

Theodora nods, silent, her incandescent gray eyes never leaving Granny's.

"You have the power of all that's good and bright in the world, child. Ravyn only has darkness, hate, and bitterness. That makes for powerful magic, but it won't hold a candle to yours."

Thunder rumbles softly, and the trees sway, spines limber, dancing in the wind howling down the mountain pass.

"A storm is coming," Theodora says, without looking away from Granny.

"You're right, a storm *is* coming," Granny replies, shaking her slightly. "And you are the only one who can give us shelter."

"What do I need to do? I'll do whatever it takes to help him." Theodora turns back to me and places both hands on the side of my head, touching her forehead to mine in a swift display of emotion.

Suddenly, the world drops away. It is only Theodora and me. My human self. My *true* self. The world around us is a black void. Only we exist here, wherever *here* is...

"Oh gods," she gasps, looking up at me. I am regaled in my princely hunting attire from Moonbright, the crest of Moonbright proud upon my chest, a crescent moon with a star. "What is happening?"

She looks down at herself, glowing like the moon, wearing a white, ethereal gown instead of her plain woolen dress. Her hair is unbound and flowing in waves across her shoulders down to her waist. I can't take my eyes off her. She looks like a goddess.

"It's our magick..." I whisper, smiling, stepping closer to her. "Our Moonbright magick. It's bringing us together, in my true form." Tears threatened to spill over my eyes. I had forgotten what it feels like to be in this human body; it feels odd to be on only two legs, even if this is a vision. It feels more real than any dream.

Theodora steps closer, gingerly touching the crest on my shoulder. "Then the stories are true?"

I nod, tucking a stray strand of silky hair behind her delicate ear. "I was hunting one day, and Ravyn enchanted me..." I trail off, lost in her eyes, not wanting to waste this precious time together talking about Ravyn Rathmore.

"Then I am here to help you, Prince Lucien, true heir to the throne of Moonbright. I will break Ravyn's curse before the rising of the red moon. Even if I have to kill Ravyn herself."

CHAPTER 12

THE GUARDIANS

THEODORA

THAT NIGHT, as I lay in bed, my heart races. My other sisters are sleeping soundly, their breathing rhythmic, breaking the silence and chill of the night.

His face haunts me.

As soon as we touched our heads together, we had instantly been transported to... where? There he stood in the mysterious black void, his golden, long blonde hair luminous, his amber eyes glowing, burning into mine. I had been in the presence of our Moonbright prince, long thought dead. A mythic figure to my clan.

Seeing him in his human form had been enchanting, exhilarating. He was a beautiful warrior, as handsome as the princes from my childhood storybooks. Tall, broad-shouldered, strong, kind...and golden, glowing like a rising moon.

I finally fall into a fitful sleep, Lucien's face drifting in and out of my mind all night. Granny is there occasionally, throwing dead rabbits at the human Lucien, who rips their flesh with canine teeth.

I awake tired, stiff, and cold, but with a resolve to train and strengthen my powers, as Granny had suggested yesterday at her cottage.

The Red Cloaks rotate rest days, and I thank the heavens today is mine. My head is full of all the things I had learned the day before, and I can't concentrate on anything. I allow my mind to drift while cooking breakfast and burn my morning porridge as I gaze out the window into the trees, wishing to get a glimpse of Lucien.

Cursing, I throw out the burned porridge and grab an apple instead, throwing on my cloak and boots and heading out into the foggy, gray morning.

I head straight into the forest, a part of the Murkfell Wood closest to the village where Ravyn's power is the weakest; it is too close to Granny's territory, and from what I gathered, Ravyn seems afraid of pushing Granny's boundaries.

I turn east, as it is the easier path, munching on my apple. I am so absorbed in my thoughts I don't realize when the trees become more twisted, closing in over my head, covering the colorless sky above.

I stop suddenly and look around, realizing I am lost.

In the distance, I can see a purple mist snaking its way along the ground, as if making its way toward me. I have wandered into Ravyn's territory without knowing it.

Ravyn has no wards to keep people out. She wants them to wander in and get stuck in her web, like a deadly spider waiting on its next meal.

Undaunted, I forge ahead, as if to meet the fell mist head on. Instead, a figure materializes from the trees, blocking my path.

She stands before me, her wheat-colored hair undulating, woven throughout with twigs and branches, as if they are sprouting from her head. Her skin is as milky as moonlight, her visage as beautiful as an angel's; but the rest of her body reveals her mystic origin. Her fingers are eerily long, capped at the ends with greenish brown talons, and her slender waist gives way to what looks like large, thick roots. She has no legs that I see.

She is a dryad, a spirit of the trees.

"Do not come this way, child," the figure says, gliding closer, like an elegant swan swimming in a lake.

"I did not mean to come this far," I tell her, stopping in my tracks. "I am lost, I'm afraid. I did not mean to come into your territory unannounced," I add, holding my hands up in surrender.

"It is not I you need to fear, Moonchild, but the darkling witch of the Murkfell and the corrupted dryads who protect her."

"I am not afraid of her," I say defiantly, standing taller and prouder. "I am a witch of the Moonbright."

The dryad looks me up and down. "Everyone who sees you knows you're a child of the Moon, young one. Your magick sings. It draws us to you."

"Us?"

The dryad steps aside, sweeping her arm to the left. There, amongst the trees, more dryads materialize, some with brown skin, some with green skin, some as pale as birch bark.

"We are the ones who are left. We are guardians here, to help warn travelers such as yourself against the Murkfell Wood. I am Dionysia, and this is my clan. Or what is left of it."

The other dryads glide closer, beginning to form a circle around me.

"Why didn't you warn me before I entered the first time? I've passed through the Murkfell before."

"We do not usually concern ourselves with the affairs of witches or humans. But our cousins, the Corrupted—they left the trees they were bound to, feeding off Ravyn's Sundark magick, perverting their gentle spirits. They are not gentle like my sisters. The Corrupted are now fierce and loyal guardians to the darkling witch. The rest of us are loyal to the light; loyal to what is good and right." The dryad's eyes spark with fury as she speaks, her anger radiating off her in waves. "Tell me child, are you familiar with Sundark magick?"

I shake my head, the dryad's eldritch eyes burning all around me in the darkness. "I have never heard of the Sundark clan at all."

The dryads drift ever closer, encircling me. I feel branches creep onto my shoulders, roots tickling my feet.

"The Sundark clan was an offshoot of the Moonbrights. But the Moonbrights banned dark moon magick a century ago. The Sundarks were becoming even more powerful they, and the Moonbrights could not have that. You know of the prophecy but not the history; your people have distorted your history. But my dear, your Moonbright clan passed a decree—any child born with the mark of dark magick—a purple caul—must be killed."

"*What?*" I gasp, not believing the kind, gentle people of Moonbright could ever perpetrate such cruelty upon any living creature, especially innocent babies. "That cannot be possible! We are a people of peace—"

"It is easy to have peace when you slay your enemy the moment they are born." Dionysia glides forward, her long roots making a sort of skirt around her as she moves. She stops right in front of my face, her leaf-green eyes boring into mine.

I hear ravens in the distance, conspiring, but I cannot break Dionysia's gaze.

"But Sundarks still live; there are ones who survived the Moonbright's execution directive. Children smuggled away, living in the darkest places, scattered to the winds as to not attract notice. This dark magick exists as the polar opposite to the Moonbright light. You are here for a reason, child. You must know this."

"That is what Granny said," I answer, looking back as I think I hear twigs snapping in the wood, as if someone is walking toward us, but I cannot see past the wall of dryads surrounding me.

"Your duty is to the people of Murkfell, but not as a Red Cloak." She lifts a long finger and touches my forehead with the pad of her finger, her long, branchlike nails resting against my face.

I suddenly see the village of Murkfell, but not in its usual, peaceful splendor.

Instead, I see ravens, hundreds upon hundreds of ravens, attacking the villagers. I can hear their screams as if I am there. The ravens are rending the flesh off bones, tearing, ripping, stabbing with their beaks. The purple mist that haunts the Murkfell traps the ones who try to run away. Bodies fall to the ground, motionless, the ravens still tearing flesh, eating it, gouging out eyes. The Corrupted dryads join the mayhem, strangling with their roots and slashing throats with the tips of their needlelike talons. Men, women, children, young and old—the minions of Ravyn Rathmore do not discriminate.

In the background Ravyn Rathmore's face suddenly comes into view, hovering in the distance, a red moon slowly rising over the horizon in an ink-black sky. Behind her is a semi-circle of more Corrupted. A direwolf is howling in the distance, a desperate, longing cry that shatters my heart.

Lucien.

I jerk my head away from Dionysia's grip, gasping for air, trying to rid my mind of that horrendous image. I swat away the tears I had not realized were falling down my cheeks. "No more, I cannot see this—"

"No, child," Dionysia said, forcefully wrapping one hand around my neck and placing her entire palm on my forehead. "You *must* see it all."

Locked in her grip, I am transported back to the blood bath wrought by Ravyn Rathmore. But this time, I see myself, running toward Ravyn, a beacon of light in the dark night.

In the vision, I thrust my hands into the air, white light emitting from my hands, clashing in the air with Ravyn's power, a black and purple mist that seems eager to devour my light. We struggle, seemingly at an impasse, our light and dark magick intertwined, moon-white and stark black streaked with purple.

"Stop! What are you doing to her?" A voice roars behind me.

Dionysia lets go, and I drop to the ground, the vision ripped from my mind. I see the dryads seep back into the trees, only Dionysia standing her ground.

It is Lucien.

He comes over to me, nudging me with his muzzle.

I stand, brushing dirt off my cloak. "I'm fine, Lucien, thank you," I tell him, marveling at him showing up and trying to protect me so fiercely.

"What were you doing to her?" Lucien demands, eye to eye with Dionysia, neither one backing down or looking intimidated by the other. Birds flutter out of Dionysia's branches as he raises his voice.

"Only showing her what will happen if she does not fulfill her destiny."

"To break the curse before the red moon?" I ask, looking from Lucien to Dionysia.

Dionysia turns, her eyes aflame. "Not just that, bright one. You must *kill* the darkling witch. And you're the only one with the power to do it. The red moon will empower her, and her magick will be no match for Granny's wards while the red moon shines. Ravyn will get into the village, there is no doubt."

"Why? Why me? Why must it be me that ends her?" I cry, exasperated with the vague talk about me fulfilling a destiny from Granny and now this dryad. "And does she really have to die? Haven't the Moonbrights done enough to her people?" Now I understand why she cursed Lucien. He is a Moonbright; either prince or peasant, Ravyn would have cursed any Moonbright who wandered into her wood that day. She wanted revenge for her people. I could understand that.

"That is for you to decipher, child. Ravyn will destroy everything in her path, including you, including Granny. She was *born* to destroy the light; it is her life's mission. Without your protection, and Granny's, the Murkfell Villagers don't stand a chance against Ravyn. The more she kills, the more her dark power grows. It will spread. It will spread and infect everything, until it leaves the world with nothing but rot and death. The world will literally drown in the infinite darkness."

"And then what happens?"

She will never stop. And then everything will become... nothing."

CHAPTER 13

THE DARKENING SKY

THEODORA

I HAD to admit I was feeling quite detached from the village and my sisters of late. While I was still in training with the Cloaks, most of my jobs were gathering in the forest and making potions, tinctures, poultices, and the like. I wasn't sure what they were training me for exactly.

With naught but a touch, I could heal anyone of just about anything.

But my mind was never here, so it was probably a good thing I wasn't treating the villagers yet.

Ever since I'd arrived, I had been living in Murkfell Village in body, but not in mind or spirit. Ever since entering the Murkfell Wood and seeing Lucien, everything else had fallen away.

The villagers had Amity, Jemma, and Cordelia.

Lucien had only me. And Granny, of course.

A few days had passed since I met the dryads on the border of the Murkfell. My next rest day was tomorrow, and I was headed to Granny's to weave my magic on the boar's heart for Lucien to take to Ravyn.

My mind raced with the revelations I had learned from Dionysia. I had hardly slept, my mind racing. I am filled with horror at the thought of my ancestors eradicating anyone born with the dark mark—a tiny birthmark in the shape of a tiny, black sun at the base of the neck. Children cannot help how they are born! It made my blood run hot all through the night, just the thought of the injustice of it all. The Moonbright clan I know and love now—including my own family—would never be capable of such atrocities.

And the thought of the Moonbrights who had escaped with their marked children, always hiding, always living in fear. It breaks my heart. That has been Ravyn's entire life. Putting up defensive walls to keep people away, so no one would find out she was a Sundark.

I find myself feeling sorry for her, despite the fact she was hellbent on killing me.

Today is another gray, rainy day, the rain pattering softly on the roof incessantly. I am making a potion when Cordelia bursts in, red hair as bright as her cloak swirling around her, her sky-blue eyes ablaze.

"Thea, come with me, NOW!" she urges, throwing my cloak before I can react, the red wool falling to a lump on the floor.

"What's wrong?" I ask, bemused, picking up my cloak and throwing it around my shoulders, grabbing my fingerless red gloves on the way out the door.

As soon as we are outside, I can see there was a fuss in the village square, a group of people circled around a prostrate figure lying on the ground.

The mix of the excited chittering of the villagers' voices mingles with the soft sound of women crying, a sobering undercurrent to the commotion.

I pull my hood up against the rain, and Cordelia pulls me toward the melee.

"Get back, get back!" Cordelia demands, pulling me into the middle of the circle, the villagers immediately heeding her stern voice.

The bodies part like water, and I finally see the dire situation of the figure on the ground.

The man lying on the ground bleeding to death is Thaddeus, the quiet and unassuming cook at the tavern, who has suffered a grievous wound to his abdomen. Blood pours from the wound, mixing with the rain, pooling under him in a muted red-black puddle, spreading out slowly into the dirt. Three large stripes gash across his torso.

Claw marks.

My heart sinks.

It can't be, I think. *He's so gentle. He would never hurt anyone.*

"It was that direwolf, Sister Theodora, look at those marks!" A young boy named Thomas exclaims, pointing at the poor man's hideous lacerations. "I seen the wolf running off right after it happened!"

"Get back, everyone, now!" Cordelia orders, shooing them away from Thaddeus, who is hyperventilating.

"Don't worry, Thaddeus," I whisper, his panicked eyes clutching at mine. I place my hands gingerly on the wound. I look at Amity, who is kneeling beside me. "Go get a tincture for pain, and one for sleep. He will need it immediately after."

Cordelia pushes the villagers back further, creating a large ring of fire around us to keep them at bay while I work.

Blood seeps through my fingers. The coppery sting in my nostrils almost distracts me from the task at hand. I close my eyes, my magick flowing through my fingers as quickly as his blood seeps through mine.

Thaddeus groans, his protestations growing louder as his wounds close from the inside out. I feel the skin stitching itself together, the magick hot in my body, flowing like fire in my veins.

With one last scream from the wounded man, I feel the final wound close.

I open my eyes, Thaddeus and I both panting from the ordeal. I wipe my brow with my apron, feeling spent.

Amity rushes over, kneels beside Thaddeus, and administers the tinctures. He is pale, much too pale.

"We need to get him home." I am trying to gather my strength, but it is waning instead. I have never felt this way after a healing.

I collapse into the dirt, Thaddeus' blood seeping slowly into my dress.

In the darkening sky, a raven circles as my world goes dark.

CHAPTER 14
CONFLICTED HEART
THEODORA

I AWAKEN SUDDENLY, shrouded in sweat. The memory of Thaddeus comes flooding back to me, and I sit up, ready to jump out of bed, when I see Jemma asleep in a chair beside my bed. Judging by the silence and the darkness that blankets the room, it is the middle of the night.

Have I been unconscious that long? It had been afternoon when I had healed Thaddeus.

I stand quietly, wrapping my dressing gown around me, and tiptoe downstairs. Walking outside, I welcome the cool night air and cold ground upon my feet. It clears my mind, cools my raging heart. I can't stop thinking about Lucien.

Lucien can't have perpetrated such violence against another human creature. I was sure of it. But Thomas said he had seen a direwolf fleeing the scene. Does another direwolf haunt these woods?

Despite my bare feet, I start walking up the hill behind the apothecary, the moonlight guiding my path. I hear a twig snap, and I twirl around to the sound to find two burning eyes at the edge of the Murkfell Wood.

A dryad?

I creep closer, feeling a chill creep up my spine. "Dionysia? Is that you?" I whisper, not wanting to cross the boundary into the forest.

Sweeping my eyes along the tree line, I see golden eyes burning in the darkness, on the edge of the forest. Lucien steps forward slightly, but Ravyn has bound him to the Murkfell Wood once more. He cannot pass the boundary of the trees into the village. I can't believe he would take the risk to be here, innocent or otherwise.

"You should go, Lucien, before the villagers get their pitchforks and torches again," I whisper, stepping closer to him, though I have to admit I feel hesitant now. "You must have been hiding well."

"Ravyn saved me with a cloaking spell at the last moment." His voice belies his tiredness despite the brightness of his eyes. "Theodora, you must know, that was not me who gravely injured that man—"

The desperation in his voice clutches at my heart, but for some reason, doubt has crept in. I can't forget Thomas, old enough not to lie or exaggerate, in a crisis. "You need to stay away from here, Lucien, before you get yourself killed." I start to back away, and Lucien tries to step forward, but the boundary stops him short. He begins to pace like a caged animal.

"Just please say you believe it wasn't me, and I will go!"

"Thea! What are you doing up there? Are you alright—" Amity's voice stops short as a shrill scream escapes instead, catching site of Lucien at the edge of the wood. "The direwolf!"

As soon as her scream peels across the village, the men on watch ring the bell in the watchtower, alerting the villagers to danger. Within seconds, a flurry of activity signals the awakened village, the hunting team pouring forth with torches, swords, saws, axes, and bows and arrows.

The words "Lucien, run!" sit on the tip of my tongue, but I cannot let the villagers know that I know who he is. Despite my conflicted heart, I don't want to see him killed. Yet at the same time, I cannot warn him.

His glowing eyes seek mine once more before he turns and dashes into the welcoming dark bosom of the Murkfell Wood.

CHAPTER 15
ONLY THE DARKNESS
LUCIEN

THE DOUBT in her eyes frightens me more than the villagers hot on my trail.

My feet pound the ground in time with my heart as I jerk suddenly to the left, heading to the small ravine of a dry riverbed. I can easily jump the span of it, but the humans will have to take to the long way, to the footbridge.

This is one time I hope to see Ravyn standing on the other side, the Corrupted fanned out around her, but no one is there. Only the darkness, which is a living thing in Ravyn's wood.

I expect the group of assailants to move as one, like a murmuration of starlings, and head to the bridge, but only half go, the rest crashing along behind me.

My left hind quarter explodes in searing pain. I glance back but don't stop, ignoring the arrow deep in my flesh.

"Get him before he jumps over the ravine!" A voice behind me to my left orders, and a flurry of arrows sails through the air, the triangular heads embedding into the tree trunks around me. I quickly prayed none of them were dryads as I gritted my teeth and sped up, my front paws leaving the earth as I hurl myself over the ravine.

Because of the arrow in my hind quarter, I land clumsily. To my right, I can see bobbing red-orange balls of light in my peripheral vision. They are heading into Murkfell, heedless of the danger lurking within. Their greed for my head as a trophy trumps even their fear of Ravyn Rathmore.

For once I purposefully head toward Ravyn's cottage, but the humans are gaining on me, the fastest of them pulling away from the herd and following me deeper into the forest.

The fiery pain in my leg is spreading now, up into my back. Poison, likely from the Red Cloaks' apothecary, coats the arrowheads. Had Theodora helped them plot my destruction? Did her elegant fingers dip the arrows herself into a deadly potion to stop my heart forever? Did she really believe I would hurt anyone?

Death was a comforting thought, for a moment. No longer tethered to this cursed lupine form. Would my spirit soar into the heavens, rejoicing, or would my very soul be bound to this place?

I know, however, my soul is bound to wherever Theodora is. For her heart now held mine captive.

I felt my body slowing, but my legs still somehow carried me toward Ravyn's cottage. She would have an antidote to whatever poison is coursing through my body. Amidst the commotion, I had not noticed Ravyn's cursed mist winding its way through the trees, garish even in the darkness. The humans, oblivious as they crash through the forest, are steps away from its fell workings. But I cannot tell them to stop. My only goal is Ravyn's cottage.

The humans press on, their shouts and cries mingled together, frenzied and chaotic. Ravyn's mist grows thicker, forming a wall. I can pass through, but the humans will surely not pass through its dark magick. As the poison works through my body, my racing heart propelling it along my veins, two ardent young men, torches and axes in hand, are hot on my tail. I can almost feel the heat from their torches. Ravyn's barrier of mist is getting closer and closer. If I can just make it beyond that boundary, the humans will not pass.

Another small volley of arrows whiz through the trees, again embedding themselves in their trunks. But one arrow makes it past the protective arms of the trees and lodges into my side. As I falter, I hear a voice, ringing through the forest.

"STOOOOOOP!"

"Hold your fire!" a man calls in the darkness, and I can't help but look back. "It is a Red Cloak!"

My legs crumple beneath me, and in the corner of my eye, I see one of the young men snarl, ready to launch his body upon mine and rain blows into my flesh with his axe. But I cannot move. I lay my head on the ground, eyelids heavy. Ravyn's mist is so close, yet so far away. I have not made it.

Something red swirls in my vision, and I hear a woman's cry, a bright flash of purple following. Bodies soar into the air, some hitting the trees with a sickening crunch. Others slam into the ground, their breath knocked from their lungs. I have not yet seen Ravyn, but no doubt she lurks undetected, working her magick in the darkness.

"Do not hurt this creature! He did not attack Thaddeus!" It is Theodora, a pleading edging into her forceful voice. She is here, protecting me. She believes me. A warmth rushes into my heart, and I wish I could stand and wrap her into my human arms to thank her. But all I can do is lie here, watching the action unfold.

One of the young men, a lumberjack by the look of him, towers over Theodora, but she does not cower or back down. "Are you in league with this beast and the fell witch of this wood, Theodora Red Cloak? You are still a stranger among us!" he growls, more beastly in his human form as I am in this one.

"He is not what you think he is!" Theodora begins, but a cackle reverberating through the night interrupts her.

The trees start to shift, slither. A vine snakes around the lumberjack's ankles with lightning speed. Cries shatter the night as the Corrupted materialize from where they had been lying in wait. Branches and vines reach for any human nearby, seeking to squeeze the life out of those who attacked their brethren.

Purple lightning unites the attacks as Ravyn bursts into the clearing, a strange, bright darkness oozing malevolence. The purple lightning shoots from her upturned palms, wrapping around the two men, restrained by vines. Their bodies jerk for a few seconds, then they are still.

Ravyn levitates in front of Theodora, hair undulating all around her, her violet eyes wild. Theodora stands her ground, palms out in a defensive stance. "My plan worked! I'm just sorry I had to kill Lucien to meet my sister."

CHAPTER 16
BREATHLESS
THEODORA

I BARELY HAVE time to register her words as I drop to my knees, my hands on his heart. I see a flash of his human face in my mind, but I drag my mind back to Ravyn and the angry mob, who have now fallen back and appear to be heading back to the village. They cannot not kill him as long as I protect him from their misplaced rage.

"Meet your sister?" I look around, and seeing no other women, I notice Ravyn's wild purple gaze fixated on me.

Ravyn throws her head back and cackles, the Corrupted that surrounded her inching backward, as if afraid of her sudden outburst.

"When Lucien first came to Murkfell, I felt his Moonbright blood. I so hoped it was my long-lost sister, but the call was not strong enough. I knew before I even saw his beautiful, tragic face. But then—" she pauses, falls to her knees in front of me, grabbing my upper arms in an iron grip. "Then, I felt it, like a lightning bolt straight to my heart. My dear, dear sister. Separated at birth. Now look at us! Together, at last!" She grabs my chin with frigid fingers and I gasp at the coldness. It seeps into my skin, the bitterest cold I've ever felt, burning and freezing me with her touch. Her purple eyes burn into mine, sparking with vitality, life...but something else.

I see the madness, feel the chaos of her mind. Tortured for years in exile, her mind had slowly shattered into millions of tiny fragments. Could anything ever repair them? I can't help but feel a small inkling of pity for this creature claiming to be my sister. But the anger rises once more as Lucien lies beside me, his breathing shallower and shallower with every passing moment.

"I understand your anger, your rage! But please, just let me heal Lucien! He never hurt you, it was those before him! Don't punish him, please!" I detest the sound of my voice, begging her to allow Lucien to live.

"If Lucien dies, it punishes those who *did* separate me from my family. So, his death has a purpose. Once he dies, he returns to his original form, and I will hang his body before the castle of Moonbright, to rend his parents' hearts out, just like they did to my poor Mother's."

I think back to my mother—Ravyn's mother, if she was telling the truth—and wonder how she hid the sorrow of losing a child all those years. Mother had told me as a child that I should have had a sister, but the gods took her while in the womb. She would go to the temple daily, lighting a candle for my sister whom I thought was never born. But instead, she had been a grieving a child who lived, but she could never see, never acknowledge as her daughter unless she wanted her hunted down and murdered.

My heart shattered, thinking of my mother grieving a lost but living child. And Ravyn, my older sister, torn from my mother's arms and hidden away just to protect her. How could I kill this pitiable creature? My own flesh and blood?

"Enough, Ravyn!"

A thunderous voice booms through the forest, shattering the crypt-like hush of the dark wood. Granny stands on the eastern side of the forest, having come down from the Windborne Pass.

Her walking stick is gripped between her gnarled fingers, her pale blue eyes sparking as wildly as Ravyn's.

"Granny! I am so happy you are here! This is a real party now!" Ravyn giggles, twirling in her black and purple dress like a young girl at a party. "Everyone is here!" She points to me, Lucien, and then Granny, in that order. "My sister, separated at birth, my Moonbright guard and familiar, and the woman who raised me, all here together!" She claps her hands, her strange violet eyes somehow both far away and frighteningly focused on the world around her.

"Wait, what? The woman who raised you?" I point to Granny, whose hawk-sharp eyes have never left Ravyn.

"For a time, yes, I tried to help this girl. But she was beyond help. I could not pull her from the darkness. So, she lived here, in this prison of my making, to keep her from harming others. But she still found a way, try as I might." Granny's voice is deep, harsh, flinty. I've never seen her like this. A storm has arisen in Granny, without any indication of when it will blow over. "But enough about that. Thea, ignore Ravyn, and heal Lucien, quickly. He is dying. As for you, Ravyn"—Granny nearly growls at Ravyn —"I will deal with you!"

Breathless, I fall my to knees again beside Lucien, my hands on his heart. As soon as our skin makes contact, I am again immersed in our shared vision, where he is human. All I see is him; his lion-blonde mane spilled around his pale face. His body is lifeless, his life force barely clinging to his mortal coil. Whether lupine or mortal, I just wanted him to live.

I am trying to mitigate the damage of the villagers' poison-tipped arrows that had pierced his direwolf body, pushing the poison away from his heart. "Lucien, you can't leave me now. I have to break the curse first!" Tears roll down my cheeks untouched, my hands never leaving Lucien.

"Thea..." Lucien's voice is a hint of a whisper, scratching against my ear. "If I die...then the curse is broken..."

"No!" I cry, the tears turning into sobs. I cannot focus

enough to heal him. The poison is so strong, there is so much. "There is another way, remember? I can break the spell, I am a Moonbright, just like you!"

Lucien's breathing is slowing. I must distance myself and focus my powers into healing him; pretend he is a villager I have never met. He needs me. I cannot be pulled into visions now, no matter how much my heart is breaking. I release an orb of light to levitate above him, and it is then I notice Dionysia and her dryads are closing in around us.

"Hurry child!" Dionysia orders, and I close my eyes and get to work, ignoring the screams and sparks of light erupting all around us.

Granny is dealing with Ravyn.

CHAPTER 17
A PRIMAL FEAR
THEODORA

THE NEXT MORNING when I leave the cottage, the village is abuzz with the events of the night before. Despite most villagers fleeing at the sight of Ravyn's poison mist and the dryads, there were enough eyes around to witness most of the events, including Ravyn's clash with Granny. I also notice more men and women guarding the outskirts of the village, eyes sharp and always searching, their axes, swords, or daggers in hand. An archer nervously checks the tautness of his bow while another secures his quiver on his back. The tension is palpable; I almost need a knife to cut through it to walk through the village.

My first stop is to check on Thaddeus, whose aunt regards me as warily as everyone had outside. A strange silence permeates the village today. Even the blacksmith's hammer is silent. I visit a few more villagers who sustained burns from Ravyn's vapor, but they seemed otherwise healthy. One young woman said she thoughtlessly retrieved one of her arrows from the foul fog, while another young man had fallen when the mob fell back, breaking his tumble with his hands before he fell on his face. It could have been much worse. They had not died the night before, they said, because of Granny's quick attention to the wounded with her strange sigils and chants. Although injured, they had at least survived.

I see Amity weaving her way down from one of the tree-houses, so I meet her as she comes down. "Amity, how do you call an emergency town meeting?"

"Ring the church bell anytime other than sunrise or sunset and people will come running, believe me. Why? Is this about last night?" Amity touches my hand, her basket looped through her arm and resting on her elbow.

I nod, looking back at the village. "If I do not address what happened last night with Lucien, I think the town might burn me at the stake for being in league with Ravyn. Then they won't stop hunting Lucien until they have his head on a spike."

Amity assures me the villagers are not nearly so backward as to burn witches, but the same could not be said when it came to Ravyn Rathmore. The villagers have always harbored much hate for her, blaming her for the lives lost over the years at the "hands of her direwolf".

"Does a village elder need to ring the bell, or may I do the honors?" I ask, gazing up at the bell tower.

"If you want to lead the meeting, you ring it yourself. Go on up, I'll help herd everyone into the church," Amity answers, heading to the village square.

Fifteen minutes later, I am standing in front of the entire village, minus anyone too sick or infirm to heed the church bell's call. The chatter ebbs and swells, wary eyes glancing at me before engaging in more heated conversations about why I called an emergency meeting.

I clap my hands, the sound echoing throughout the church. The babble recedes, all eyes now glued to my face. I feel the blood rush up to my face, not accustomed to addressing such a large audience. But Lucien's face flashes in my mind's eye, and I find my courage—and my voice—once more.

"Good people of Murkfell, I have called this meeting to address the events of last night. There are things you must know,

for your own safety, that have nothing to do with the direwolf—"
I begin, but the voices swell once more, cresting like an immense
wave threatening to break and drown me.

The church doors fling open, and there stands Cordelia, a
ball of flame in her hands burning as brightly as her jade-green
eyes. "Let her speak! Or so help me, I will set this chapel
aflame!"

Gasps from mothers and tiny yelps from their young children
pepper the air as Cordelia strides in, Jemma, Amity, and Elwen
behind her, red cloaks whipping around them, their elemental
powers roaring around their cupped hands in a rare display of
power. They join me at the front of the church, their counte-
nances fierce as they stare down the villagers.

"Theodora Mourningbeam is in league with that devil witch
and her hound from hell!" An old man stands amidst a chorus of
agreement erupting around him, pointing a grubby, knotty finger
at me, his hat clutched in the other tanned and leather-worn
hand. "She's no Moonbright, she's a Sundark come out of hiding,
you mark my words!"

"Check her for the mark!" A woman's voice now, crying out
from the back of the church, and roar ensues in agreement.

A burly woodsman pushes out of the crowd standing at the
back of the church and stomps up the aisle, his eyes dark and
murderous. Before he can even get halfway, however, Cordelia
shoots a warning spark at his feet, and jumps back, cursing.

"If you come any further, Ferson, you'll burn faster than dead
wood in summertime," Cordelia smirks, taking a step toward the
woodman, who quickly takes a step back.

Amity flicks her palms up, a blast of wind hitting the man,
whose face crumples into a scowl, eyes burning in anger. "It
would be a shame if a little breeze fanned those flames. An
inferno would envelop you in seconds."

Jemma giggles, holding up her hands, sparkling water
swishing between the two. "No one else will burn, as they will be
too wet. But not you!"

"Listen to me!" Time is growing short, and my patience wears thin. "Last night, you all tried to kill the direwolf, believing he attacked Thaddeus. But it was Ravyn Rathmore who attacked him, not the wolf! The wolf has never attacked another human ever; it has always been Ravyn!"

Voices begin to swell, but I quell their indignation, holding up my hands again. "The wolf is not our problem, it is Ravyn! The wolf is her victim, not an agent of death. He is a human, cursed to live as a direwolf. He has never hurt any of you, but you have done nothing but torment him for years. I can help break his curse as a Moonbright witch, but first I must deal with Ravyn."

"How do you know all this about the wolf?" Ferson asks, his face still red as embers. "You must know dark magick like Ravyn!"

"The human trapped inside the direwolf is a Moonbright just like me!" The words are out of my mouth and much louder than I had expected. Again, the mob falls silent, so I continue while I still can. "He just needs my help to break the spell so he can be human again, that is all he wants."

A wizened old woman with skin like onyx and eyes like golden suns shuffles up to me, takes my hands. All eyes in the church are upon us.

"Is it he, child? The one in the prophecy? Is he the lost prince of Moonbright?" Her voice is thin and delicate, like old paper or moth's wings.

Tears fill my eyes as I see his beautiful face in my mind, eyes like a rising moon, when it is plump and serene and golden. I nod, clutching the old lady's hands tighter. Her countenance is so unusual, with the contrast of her bright eyes and night-sky skin. I cannot remember her name, nor her face, despite her striking visage. But I strike it from my mind as the crowd reacts to the news. In the midst of the din I could make out "lost prince" and "Moonbright" mingling with "curse" and "prophecy".

"So what if the enchanted wolf is really a prince? That

doesn't affect me none." Fergus crosses his arms, his massive muscles straining against his woolen shirt. "The way I see it, if you're gone Miss Mourningbeam, we will all be safe again. Ravyn keeps to herself as long we don't go into her wood."

"I will tell you why all of this matters to you, woodsman. Because I have seen a vision from the dryad Dionysia." The church falls to a hush with the mention of Dionysia's name. The villagers both fear and respect her, as she and her kind help protect the village from Ravyn's foul, dark magick. "It is me she is after, but after the vision I saw, I believe she will attack the village out of spite. Or it will officially signal her reign of terror. On the night of the red moon, everyone will be vulnerable. She might attack the village even if I am not here, and she will not stop with Murkfell Village or Windborne! Her destruction will spread like a wildfire, killing everything in its path. I can help you take back your wood, take back your freedom! Ravyn Rathmore has had you all in shackles for years!"

Nods in agreement from a smattering of people in the pews. At least some people seemed to have the courage to stand against Ravyn.

"All this trouble started when you came to this village, Moonbright, Sundark, whatever you are! An abomination, I call all of you!" The woodman Ferson still stands in the aisle, unable to move forward but unwilling to take his seat once more. His finger points at us, the Red Cloak sisters, standing elbow to elbow at the front of the church. "Even if you are not in league with Ravyn Rathmore, the village must exile Theodora Mourningbeam as she is an immediate threat to our safety!"

The crowd's one voice surges again, although this time I can hear dissenters raising their voices in my defense.

"Enough!" Ezekiel, the old woodman-turned-toymaker, shuffles to the front of the church. Voices silent, eyes fall upon him expectantly. As a village elder and lifelong Murkfell resident, he commands respect. "You all know the prophecy! A Moonbright witch will end Ravyn's might—and Theodora is the one! She is not in league with the Sundark, but as a Moonbright, it is only her magick that can stop Ravyn. The red moon rises tomorrow night, and according to the prophecy, this is when Theodora's magick can stop Ravyn and end the curse of the Murkfell Wood once and for all! No more direwolf, no more poisonous mists, no more Corrupted! No more Ravyn Rathmore! And that poor lost prince gets his freedom."

"What do we do? How do we fight against Ravyn and her minions when we have no magick of our own?" A young woman with a babe clutched to her breast calls out from the front row. "How do we protect our vulnerable? The elderly, the infirm, the children?"

I nod, happy that Ezekiel has at least made them listen to reason, if only for a moment. "Excellent question, Lily. Starting tomorrow, I believe everyone who cannot protect the village in case of attack should head over the pass and seek sanctuary in Windborne. We will send messengers over tonight so the village can begin preparing. Everyone who can stand with us will stay in Murkfell. We will need defenses around the entire perimeter of the village. Archers, we need all of you to take down her ravens from the sky, and woodsmen—you will attack the Corrupted with your axes. We do not want to use fire unless absolutely necessary, so we won't burn down the village."

"Good plan, but what about Ravyn's poisonous mist? How do we keep that from killing us all?" Cordelia asks, crossing her arms over her chest. "That is going to be a problem."

"I must ask Granny for help with that issue. But I am hoping she only comes after me and leaves the village alone."

Cordelia scoffs, emerald eyes flashing. "She will attack the village as a lark just to get at both you and Granny, so stop being so naïve."

"From what I know of Ravyn, she can only cast one type of magick at once. She must focus her control on both her ravens and her dryads; if she is controlling both, she cannot cast her mist, and vice versa. We must exploit this weakness." Ezekiel's voice is raspy and weak, but when he speaks, everyone hushes and leans forward to hear him. "People of Murkfell, hear me now! We must begin preparations immediately if we are to save our village, our way of life. The power of the red moon is already rising. And so is the power of Ravyn Rathmore."

CHAPTER 18

THE GATHERING STORM
THEODORA

Thea,

Lucien is healing well but still weak. He is safe with me. All is well. Come to me when you can.

-Granny

I sigh, holding the scrap of paper in my hands. Villagers prepare for Ravyn's arrival. They should have been preparing for the Red Moon Festival instead. I do not know when I will have time to trek up the pass to Granny's to see her or Lucien. Tonight, the festival begins—which means the red moon will rise, and Ravyn will be coming. I thank the messenger, who in return thanks me for the coin I press into his hand before he scampers off into the twilight.

All those who could not defend the village in case of attack are assembling near the bridge, wagons carrying supplies on the fringe of the encircled group. Anxiety churned in my stomach; they should have left much earlier. In a clearing beside the apothecary, Elwen instructs villagers on how to make stretchers out of fabric and tree branches to carry the sick and infirm, while Cordelia helps make torches to line the perimeter of the village. Elwen is helping make bandages at the tailor's shop, and

Jemma works her magick in the apothecary making the strongest healing potions known to the Red Cloaks.

I wrap my cloak tighter around my shoulders and head to the village center, where Ezekiel is deep in a heated discussion with the throng of elders, who have amassed outside of his shop. The blacksmith's hammer swings away, almost in time to the *thwock* of axe blades as men and women practice throwing hatches and axes at nearby trees. I silently hoped they would not mistake the dryads for Ravyn's Corrupted and accidentally hit one of our much-needed allies.

There were no preparations for the Red Moon Festival, however. The children would have to enjoy the festival in Windborne tonight, as there was no other choice. At least in Windborne, the children could forget about the scary witch threatening their village and enjoy a once-in-a-lifetime event complete with delicious food, games, and entertainment of all kinds, like singers, acting troupes, and acrobats. I wondered if Ezekiel would still perform his puppet show about Ravyn's prophecy. The Murkfell Wood did not heavily influence Windborne's lore, since their village did not border that cursed forest.

My eyes search the east toward Windborne, waiting for a glimpse of the red moon rising that will bloody the horizon with its abyssal rays. With relief I see the caravan finally begin their ascent up the pass. It is solemn, quiet, almost like a funeral procession. Their torches pinprick the sapphire blue of the twilight evening. The night is so beautiful it is hard to believe anything bad could happen.

And now, with everyone occupied, I can sneak away into the Murkfell and bring the fight to Ravyn, heading her off before she can even think of coming for the villagers. I made sure they were ready in case Ravyn did bring the fight to them; but if my plan worked, the villagers would not see battle this night. I had told no one of my plan to sneak into the Murkfell Wood to attack Ravyn alone, unawares. I have had no time to learn exactly how to use my powers against Ravyn; I have only used them to heal, never to harm. But I have to face her, so I muster up the courage to trust myself, that I will know what to do when the time comes.

It is all about saving Lucien. He is all that matters.

Taking a deep breath to gather my resolve, I turn and head west, straight into the heart of the Murkfell Wood.

"Just where do you think you are going, young lady?"

The voice arrests my steps, and I whirl around to face Granny, hooded in a deep blue cloak, eyes ablaze within its dark shadows.

"Granny!" I exclaim, feeling the heat race up to my cheeks like wildfire. "What are you doing down in the valley? You should stay up on the mountain with Lucien until all this is over. Where is he, by the way?"

"He lingers on the other side of the river so he can stay in within the boundaries of my wards. Why did you not come? We haven't much time to prepare for what may happen tonight."

"I do not plan on slaying my sister, no matter how twisted her mind is."

Granny scoffs, a long tuft of silvery hair lifting slightly with the force of her breath. "Then you will die tonight, and so will many other innocent people."

"I will at least do what I can to reason with her! I just want her to release Lucien from his curse. I am her sister, maybe she will listen—"

Granny throws back her head, a cackle issuing from the almost faceless hood of the cloak. "All the more reason why she won't listen! You are a Moonbright; she has hated your clan since she formed her first memories. Sister or no, you will die tonight if you think she will spare you."

I sigh, grow quiet. I had done nothing personally to Ravyn. I just wanted to help Lucien and her, to help put their many wrongs right.

"When the time comes, your magick will know what to do.

Trust in your magick; it is all that can guide you through this dark night."

I nod, sighing. People are still crossing the bridge, the torchlight like dozens of tiny suns weaving in and out of the darkness. "I want to see Lucien," I say, nodding in the direction of the bridge. The wards still speckle the air, the sigils sparkling in the torchlight as villagers walk by. But tonight, the wards will mean nothing if Ravyn wants to get past them. Her magick will be stronger than Granny's, if only for tonight.

A strong breeze slams into Granny's face, her hood falling back. The trees sway and bend, dancing in time to the wind's song. I notice dark clouds on the horizon in the last light of the day.

"Looks like a storm is brewing," I comment, gesturing toward the lightning already zigzagging across the sky. "I don't know if that will help our cause or hurt it."

"It's a storm alright," Granny says, gazing toward the clouds. "And its name is Ravyn Rathmore."

CHAPTER 19
RED MOON RISING
LUCIEN

FATE DANGLES ON A THIN, golden thread. My life is in the hands of another. It always seems to be.

As a prince, my life was never my own. I had belonged to my country. As a direwolf, I have been in Ravyn's control. And on the night of the angry mob, both Ravyn and Thea stopped the raving villagers from surely killing me; later, Granny held sway over life and death, mitigating most of the damage from the poison after Thea's rapid healing in the forest. Without all three of them—even Ravyn—I would be dead. And according to Granny, Dionysia also deserved my gratitude.

And once again, I cannot control the outcome of my fate tonight. I will either be released from the witch's bonds and regain my humanity or stay trapped, still writhing within Ravyn's talons like the helpless prey that I am.

"I am going to find Theodora. She should have been here by now. The hour grows late." Granny walks into the small clearing in front of her cottage where I sit, gazing out toward the village below. Twilight has descended, tinting the sky in a calming shade of lapis. I cannot see it from here but knowing it is there—that Theodora is there—comforts me somehow. "I am afraid I will be too late to stop her."

"From going after Ravyn first? You know Thea will want to head her off, lure her away from the village if she can. Ravyn will relish killing those innocent people because she knows it will torment Thea. I've been with her for years, I know how her mind works."

Granny pats my shoulder. "Stay here. You must not get involved in this fight. It is between the sisters."

"But I am also a Moonbright," I protest, but Granny holds up her hand.

"You are a prince, not a witch. Have you ever performed any kind of magick? No, you never had to do anything for yourself," she continues before I can answer. "You never *needed* to use magick. Thea was born quite poor, so she has always had to use her magick to help support her family as a healer. Her magick "muscles" are much stronger than yours, so to speak. You must crawl before you can walk. And you're not even crawling yet, Lucien."

I sigh, not saying anything. She is right, as always. Theodora knows how to take care of herself. I have to trust in her, believe that she can break my curse. I have no other choice.

"I am going," Granny snaps the hood of her cloak up against the wind, which is picking up as a storm gathers. "Stay here and stay out of trouble." She turns and gives me a knowing look before she disappears down the pass.

I wait a few minutes before I head out in the opposite direction of Granny. I slink through the trees, weaving in and out of shimmering sigils from Granny's wards in complete silence. The further off the path I go, the lighter the sigils become, until I am out of them completely. I head to higher ground to bypass the villagers snaking their way across the bridge and up the pass. If Thea is going to put herself in danger for my sake, I cannot sit on my haunches and do nothing.

I run along the edge of the forest beside the village, close enough to see but not close enough to attract attention. The village has a secure perimeter of torches and guards, their shoulders taut with anxiety, their stances stiff. Silhouettes move among the houses in the trees, restless archers checking the tautness of their bows and the sharpness of their arrows. It is oddly quiet, as if Ravyn has also cast a spell of silence, stealing the voices from their throats.

I see Red Cloaks moving about the village, one here, one there, but none of them are Thea. Is she already in Murkfell Wood, searching for Ravyn? Ravyn could be anywhere.

And then, like a raindrop falling into a pond so still it looks like glass, a solitary scream ripples down the pass and into the forest, disturbing its pristine stillness.

Oh no. The last of the villagers on the pass, still trying to get to Windborne. Then a rush of caws as ravens swoop out of the trees, previously unseen and unheard. Voices yelling from above. The archers in the treehouses call orders to one another, shooting upwards at the sky instead of at the dryads. *The ravens.*

Then a shriek from the forest's edge, then another, and another. Movement behind the guards, and then all around the perimeter, the trees are suddenly alive, gnarled black branches attempting to strangle, gouge, cut—destroy—anything in their path. *The Corrupted.*

I hear a low rumble, a collective growl as the woodsmen surge forth, brandishing axes and bravado, their blades sinking deep into the bark-flesh of the dryads. Their screeches pierce my ears, sharp as blades.

Then I see it, the purple mist, snaking among the trees, creeping toward the church. With most of the village populace gone, there should have been no one in the church seeking sanctuary.

Until a man bursts through the church doors, the body of a woman in his arms. "Help her! Please! Help her! That witch has blinded my wife!"

I have never heard such horror, such desperation in someone's voice before. My hackles stood on end, a rage rising in me like never before. The Red Cloaks are using the church as a makeshift hospital, but they may as well be ducks in a barrel. And I still have no idea where Thea is. But I have to warn the people in the church.

Forgetting everything, the last decade of hiding, of fear, of silence, I roar into the village center, my voice echoing among the majestic trees. "Get to the trees! Get to higher ground! Now!"

The loggers ignore me, still hacking away at the dryads. A few bodies lie crumpled, motionless. I race to the church, repeating my pleas from before. A Red Cloak sister, her eyes flashing emerald amidst a cascade of night-dark hair, looks out of the door, and seeing me, and the mist, her eyes widen in horror. Surely she knows it is me trying to help?

The world is chaos. I am not sure who to help first. The dryads, the ravens, the mist, all at once. The screams are everywhere around me, like a living creature with an electric pulse. The power of the red moon is in Ravyn's favor now. Her power might be limitless. But so could Theodora's.

Through the towering trees, I glimpse Windborne Pass, torchlight flitting to and fro from the tumult between the villagers and ravens. An unnatural red seeps along the edges of the horizon, a bloody wound slashed into the falling darkness.

The red moon is rising.

❧❀❧

THEODORA

Granny and I both hear the solitary scream at the same time, both whirling back around in the direction of the village.

"What was that?" I whisper, hoping it was just a wild animal screeching in the night. But no. Screams cascade like waterfalls, the sounds growing as I bolt toward the village, my feet already carrying me back before the danger barely registers. I risk a glance back at Granny, who impatiently waves her hand as if to say, "Go on, don't wait on me, girl!"

As I break through the trees, I see it.

The red moon. I can see it, rising through the pass.

Energy surges within me. I grit my teeth, running past the apothecary and our quarters, past the grist mill. The path from the apothecary to the village square has never seemed so lengthy. It's as if it stretches on and on, never-ending, like in a nightmare.

The village center is empty, and Ravyn's fell mist surrounds the church. I hear voices calling my name from above, and I look up at the snug houses built in the trees where archers are dealing with Ravyn's conspiracy of ravens. The arrows are swift and true, but the horde seems to be endless. Through the candlelit windows I see huddles of tense shoulders and fearful eyes watching the events outside. Refugees from the pass, who did not make it into Windborne in time.

A few lumberjacks still brawl with the last of the Corrupted that have not fled, the fight in favor of the woodsmen. But judging by the corpses on the ground, not all of them had been so lucky. The archers beckon me up into the towering trees, but I cannot tend to the wounded or seek my own safety. I have to find Ravyn and Lucien.

"Lucien!" I yell into the darkness, my voice breaking at the end. "Lucien!!"

A hulking dark shadow emerges from around the back of the church. The eyes, glowing gold in the darkness.

"Lucien!" His name is less a word and more of a relieved sigh as leaves my lips, throwing my arms around his neck, burying my face in his fur. "I was so worried about you! But where is Ravyn?" I ask, determined, sliding down from his neck and landing firmly on the ground.

A thunderbolt of pain arrests my body, like lightning coursing through my veins. As the ground rises to meet my awaiting body, purple tinges my vision.

Ravyn's maniacal laugh dances upon the air. "Does that answer your question, dear sister?"

CHAPTER 20
THE CHOICE
THEODORA

"STOP THIS MADNESS, Ravyn! These people are innocent! They have nothing to do with us!"

Lucien's voice drifts through the fog of pain. I gasp, roll over to my knees. I grit my teeth. In spite of the knives stabbing through my veins from Ravyn's attack, it was time for her to meet Moonbright magick.

I am on my feet again, the red moon floating in an ink black sky. There are no stars. Lucien nudges me all over with his cold nose to see if I am alright, but I pay no mind. Vaguely I hear the cries of the archers as they volley their arrows, again and again. The Corrupted have slithered back into the night, for now, and the woodcutters stumble over to begin their ascent up to the treehouses. Time is moving like molasses in winter.

The church doors fling open, and Amity stands silhouetted against the candlelight, palms in front of her. The trees around her sway to her command, loose dust and debris form tiny twisters. Her target is dispelling the mist from around the church, but it stands resolute against Amity's magick.

I shrug off my cloak, and it falls to my feet like a puddle of blood. The world is tinged in crimson as the red moon climbs higher in the sky, over the mountains.

I feel almost feral now, my body healing itself, albeit painfully, from Ravyn's Sundark magick. I bite my lip to keep from grimacing. But my magick is overtaking hers inside my body; my hands grow warm with it, my fingers tingle.

A roar escapes from my throat unbidden, and it rips into the red night, joining the other cries of the villagers. The voices grow stronger, as if there are more people joining in the fight on the pass, but I must keep my eyes on Ravyn. From what Lucien has told me, I know Ravyn's magick far outmatches my own; she is cunning, wily, and can disappear and reappear with no warning. I have no such powers. But I have something she does not.

I have love. I have hope. I have kith and kin.

My arms stiffen in front of me, and white Moonbright healing magick erupts from my palms with a force like never before. I feel the red moon's power gnawing away at my insides, and it had to come out before I exploded with it. It strikes Ravyn's chest and she flies backward, landing with a crash on the sizeable pile of firewood outside of Ezekiel's workshop.

With a maniacal laugh, she is up in seconds, her wild violet eyes almost sparking embers into the night. Is this really my sister? Entwined in my hate for her is also a stabbing pity that I feel deep inside. It tugs at my heart, weighs me down. But my desire to save Lucien and help the villagers lightens the load and keeps me on my feet.

"You have no idea what you are doing, sister!" Ravyn exclaims as we circle each other, our hands in front of us in defensive gestures, our magick slithering in and around our hands like ethereal snakes. Hers purple, mine golden, so different, yet still so alike.

As the mountain comes into view, I see figures cresting the top of the pass from the Windborne side, then pause, arrows pointed to the sky. Windborne archers. I see a movement in my peripheral vision, and as my eyes flick back to Ravyn, she is twirling one arm in the air, and her mist encircles the village square, trapping me inside it. I knew better than to look away.

She, however, trains her eyes on me with hawk-like focus, never breaking my gaze. Yet she seems far away at the same time. The red moon is eating away at her mind while also fueling her magick. The darkness overtakes her mind. Did she still have a soul for the darkness to claim?

Ravyn is levitating, light as air. Her violet dress dances in the gusts from Amity, who still tries to dissipate the mist from the churchyard. I do not see the other sisters. My eyes pass over Lucien, who can only watch with glowing eyes from the distance. Even he cannot intervene. But despite his calm exterior I feel his worry.

My mind fragments, pulling me from the moment at hand. A creaking sound and Lucien's cries bring me back to myself just in time to see a tree uproot and tip over. I bolt just in time, the tree crashing outside of the square thanks to Amity's wind guiding the other way.

"Focus, Theodora! The red moon is pulling you away from yourself, girl! Remember who you are and why you are here!"

Granny.

Even Ravyn turns at her voice, her former guardian. Does she still harbor a love for Granny, or did she ever?

I take the opportunity and swing my right arm in an arc in front of my body, the blinding moon white power slamming Ravyn from the side. She crashes through the window of the tailor shop, glass skittering over the wooden deck outside. The dress dummy topples out of the window, dragging torn linen with it as Ravyn clatters onto the floor with a high-pitched yelp. Needles, spools of thread, and bolts of fabric topple on top of her, but she bats it all away with a screech. Her unbound hair is a wild, tangled mess, like a bird's nest fallen from its tree. In seconds she is through the window again, stomping towards me, her teeth gritted in such fierce determination it seems as if they will break and explode from her mouth in tiny fragments.

Ravyn's arm lashes an ethereal violet whip, and I scream as my left arm sears in pain, as if a thousand red-hot brands are pressing upon my skin. That damned mist! Pieces of fabric from the sleeve of my dress have simply disintegrated, leaving my arm bare, raw, and flaming red. But my body will take care of the rest and heal itself. Right now, I have to take care of Ravyn.

As my magick leaves my fingertips, Ravyn's meets mine, and we struggle in vain against one another at first, at a stalemate, our magick locked together, equally opposing forces. The red moon hangs over heads. How can the night pass so quickly? As we circle each other once again, I glimpse Granny in the church-yard, sigils dancing over her head, her staff tapping the ground in rhythm. She will pave a way for the wounded to get through if she can outwit Ravyn's magick on this doomed night.

I feel Ravyn's power overtaking mine, but with one final push, I send everything I have to hit Ravyn. Sweat pours down my face and into my eyes, and despite the skin on my arm heal-ing, I still feel the poison from her mist working its way through my body, slowing me down. The poison seems to be working faster than my body can heal itself.

Ravyn barely falters as the attack hits, and instead she laughs at my feeble attempt.

"Thea! Incoming!" I hear Granny's voice, and she throws something into the village square, inside the ring of purple. It clatters on the dirt at my feet. A bottle of potion. I grab it up and gulp it down, throwing the bottle at Ravyn's face to distract her. She swats it away like a fly, laughing.

"While you were living the good life in Moonbright as a little healer, I lived out in the darkness of these forests, honing my magick. You're nothing to me, little sister. No more worrisome than a cloudy day." She shoots small little balls of magick at me now, pelting my skin, as if taunting me.

I can barely keep up, and some of the projectiles get by my defenses and hit me, knocking me back. But I can't let her win.

In the span of a second, Ravyn blinks out of existence in front of me, then reappears immediately to my left, then to my right, then behind me. As soon as I catch up, she's gone again.

And then my feet are off the ground and I'm sailing through the air with what feels like a cannonball in my gut. Ravyn tosses me like a rag doll through the air, and I explode through the doors, which had again been shut. My body sails right through the wood, and I crash onto the aisle, sliding on my back, breathless, before landing right at Cordelia's feet.

"There you are," she says, unconcerned by my violent entrance. "I thought you would never get here. Now, it's time to get to work, sisters."

<hr />

WITH SEVERAL BOTTLES thrust into my hands, Elwen instructs me to drink each one in turn, her hand supporting mine as I tip them back. "Hurry, Thea, Granny can only keep her busy for so long." She gazes outside with worried eyes. The color reminds me of the deep green of the leaves in summer. "We have to keep Ravyn out the church, there are still wounded trapped in here!"

I nod, Amity and Cordelia helping me to my feet. Jemma stays behind the pulpit with the wounded, ready at a moment's notice to protect them. I already feel the potions working, helping my own body along in its healing process against Ravyn's poison. Her Sundark magick is overpowering my own, but I cannot admit that, not now. I sprint outside, ignoring the feeling of burning cold running through my veins. Even the warped sorcery of that cursed moon was not helping me defeat her.

A Moonbright will defeat Ravyn. If not me, then who?

I let anger fuel me as I stalk across the churchyard, back to the square, where Granny has backed Ravyn into the circle of mist once again, away from the church, but Ravyn suddenly bolts, running down the forest path in the direction of the apothecary.

All the while, the moon continues making its journey across the pitch-dark sky to the west. I cannot let this moon set without breaking the curse.

I dash after her, feeling Lucien in my wake, and he quickly catches up to me. "She is running instead of projecting, that means her energy is waning as the moon sets. This is a good thing!"

Or she could be tricking us. I choke down the words and nod, my eyes scanning the dark path ahead of us. "Lucien, I don't see her! Where did she go?"

We both stop on the path, looking around, feeling exposed. It feels unusually claustrophobic, the blood-tinged darkness closing in on us. No other sounds issue from the forest; no insects, no animals, nothing. The silence, it is eerily unnatural.

I take a step to move Lucien off the path into the woods, but I fall over with a yelp, feeling a sharp pain in my right elbow as roots and vines wrap around my legs, dragging me away from Lucien. I feel warmth running down my arm onto my wrist and onto the palm of my hand.

"Lucien!" I scream, but Ravyn is hurling her body through the air at mine like a wildcat pouncing on its prey. Just like a smart apex predator, she had lured me away from the safety of the town square to the darkness of the Murkfell.

I am so surprised she is attacking me physically I react too late, and my attack misses. She rolls over on top of me, her hands around my throat.

"Why did *you* get to stay?" Her voice is more growl than voice, more feral than human. Her skin, close up, almost has a grayish hue; what should have been beautiful features are marred by her blind rage. I kick and scramble, trying to unlock her fingers while simultaneously kicking off the Corrupted's roots and vines that were restraining me. "You had a home, you had people to care about you, to love you, while I..." she tightens... "was..." she tightens again... "...abandoned!" She screams the last word, her hands tight enough to break my windpipe. I can no longer even gasp for air; the world turns black.

Ravyn shrieks again, this time in pain. My eyes fly open as she is violently yanked backward by her hair, and I take the sweetest breath of air I have ever taken, which is soon replaced by hacking coughs.

Dionysia holds a kicking, screaming Ravyn by the hair, her other dryad maidens holding her arms and legs. I can tell it will not be for long. Her dark sorcery, still amplified by the slowly sinking moon, will soon overtake the dryads and harm them. By the looks of their torn branches and scarred bark, they are the ones who caused the Corrupted to fall back earlier, ceasing their attacks on the woodcutters.

"Just let her go, Dionysia, before she harms you any further." My voice is a croak, muffled by the density of the forest and Ravyn's death grip. My hand grips my throat as if it will help.

Ravyn thumps to the ground but is up again before I can blink. Our arms locked, we spin up, up, up, before I have time to realize what is happening. She slams me against the trunk of a towering old tree, her forearm against my throat. "How will you save him?"

"Wh-what?" I gasp, barely getting the word out. She presses harder into my throat.

"The only way to free Lucien of his curse is to kill him now. You are no match for me, Theodora Mourningbeam! So, he can live as a direwolf, forever with me in Murkfell, or die he can tonight. Either way...I win!"

Ravyn's twig-like fingers are around my throat again, and she slams me into the ground, right at Lucien's feet.

"Make a choice, sister." She has one hand on my throat, the other hovers near Lucien's, a wispy ball of purple in her palm.

"Ravyn, let her go!" Lucien cries, but his voice is in the background, drowned out by the heartbeat pounding in my ears.

"Let him live," I gasp, "but I will take his curse. He does not have to die. I take his curse. I take his curse."

The last thing I remember is Lucien's desperate, horrified howl echoing into the empty crimson night.

EPILOGUE
LUCIEN

THIS BODY FEELS STRANGE, even a month later.

My legs feel too long, my equilibrium askew. I see the world through very different eyes than before Ravyn enchanted me. Before, the world was awash in a rosy glow, full of hope, life, and a bright future that awaited me as the reigning heir of the Moonbright kingdom.

But now. Now, through eyes stained by Ravyn's Sundark magick and the harsh truth about my clan, the world seems a much darker place.

A shadow passes over the window, and I stumble out of bed, knocking over the washstand in my haste, water splashing onto the floor. I ignore it, snatching the curtain back from the window. Granny will complain about her floors, but it will have to wait. She is here.

She waits under the canopy of trees behind Granny's house. My beautiful, haunted Theodora.

Though her body is a stranger, her eyes are still the same luminous gray moon they were when she was human. Now, she sits on her haunches, her melancholy eyes piercing my heart as I tear through the trees to greet her. Her eyes are still jolting to see; frighteningly human eyes trapped in a direwolf's body. Was this how I looked to her? The sad human gazing from between the bars of a wolfish prison?

But even as a wolf, she is stunning, her sleek black fur glinting with tiny prisms in the dappled morning sun.

I throw my arms around her, my face buried in her fur. She whimpers in my ear. I know her fear: that of succumbing into that lupine nightmare and never awakening. Like me in the early days of Ravyn's enchantment, she has refused to eat much in the first weeks of her newfound imprisonment. The human mind revolts at the thought of hunting and tearing into raw flesh. She is resisting the hunger, the desire to eat and revulsion at the process. I know, because I resisted too. But her body—and mind —grow weak.

"Thea, you must eat. Granny and I set traps for you yester-day. Let us go check them."

A few moments later, bow and quiver slung over my shoulder, we near the pass. Thea looks at me with eager eyes, but I shake my head. "Thea, I know you miss your Red Cloak sisters, but it cannot be helped. The villagers will still fear you, even if they know it is still you in there. As Ravyn's direwolf, you represent a magick they do not understand, so it is natural for them to fear it. And they will be more frightened if they know you are not bound to the Murkfell Wood, as I was."

The Murkfell Wood stands quiet now, Ravyn's cottage aban-doned, her minions gone with her. The wood is slowly healing itself, after Granny swept through and "cleansed" it with her magick. Where Ravyn has gone, no one knows, but I can't help but look over my shoulder now and then, expecting her to appear. But I feel it in my marrow; Ravyn still lives.

Thea has not spoken since she took my curse. I remember feeling that I had lost my voice for a few days after my enchant-ment, but I soon found it, if for nothing else than to feel Ravyn's ire. And now, even when we touch, we do have the shared visions of both of us in human form like before. Ravyn might be gone, but Theodora's curse remains.

I thought that by killing Ravyn, by opening her throat before she could cast that fateful spell, that everything would return to normal. That I would return to my human form and not have to die. That Theodora would live by my side as my Moonbright queen, and we would seek to pay our debt to the Sundarks, who deserve to live in the light.

But I was too late. As soon as the words escaped Theodora's lips, the spell began.

I take his curse. I take his curse.

The words thrummed in time to my heart, ceaselessly echoing in my ears.

As I had lunged for Ravyn, my heart shattered into a thousand pieces as Theodora's screams ripped through the night, her body convulsing and contorting. Memories of my own changing slashed at my mind as I roared, heaving my weight toward Ravyn's slight form. But instead of contacting with Ravyn's flesh, I had flung my clumsy body to the ground, already in human form; and Ravyn had used the last bit of her strength to disappear, leaving only her projected spirit behind to mingle her laughter with Theodora's cries as the red moon melted into the dark horizon.

And now, like then, Ravyn is the only one we know who can undo the spell.

"We cannot know how the red moon changed the enchantment; the moon had not quite set when the spell was cast, so its magick has its hold on Theodora, just like Ravyn's Sundark magick does. Only time will tell. And in the meantime, we must find Ravyn."

Granny's words echo in my mind in time to our steps as we head to the first trap. Granny had kept me away for days after Theodora's changing, working her ancient magick in private, as she is wont to do.

But still, a month later, Thea will not speak, and darkness holds court in her eyes.

Theodora's head jerks to the left, toward the forest path, her ears pricked. My human ears seem almost deaf compared to my former razor-sharp auditory skills. I hear nothing. Her tail drops slightly, and she runs further to the right, away from the path. She beckons me to come by nodding her head, but I stay, finally hearing horse's hooves. I duck behind the nearest tree, motioning for Thea to stay where she is. They have come the long way around the Murkfell Wood; they have no idea Ravyn no longer holds sway over that forest. The messenger is heading to Windborne. I take a look back at Thea's anxious eyes, then head to the path. The hurried pace of the horse's hooves displays a haste that only bad news brings.

I signal to the messenger and bow, and she slows the horse, surprised at my sudden appearance. With a start, I see the crest of Moonbright upon her tabard.

"My lady, what news? May I be of any assistance?"

She eyes me suspiciously, bow and quiver slung over my shoulder, then looks ahead of her, as if debating. Then making a decision, she finally speaks, her horse stamping impatiently.

"There has been an attack on Moonbright, sir. We are calling in reinforcements from all nearby villages. The inhabitants of Murkfell are arming up as we speak. I must away, sir, to Windborne, if you will excuse me!" The messenger is off before she even finishes speaking, and I am racing back into the thick of the trees to alert Theodora, but of course she has heard every word.

She stands, her eyes even more troubled than before. I know she is thinking of her family, as I think of mine. I wonder who is dead, and who is alive.

And is it Ravyn who is attacking? It would be the perfect time for her to attack, with Theodora in direewolf form.

"Lucien!" Granny is stomping her way through the thicket with her staff, flowers falling out of her hair from the force of her steps. "Have you heard? The village is abuzz!"

"Is it her, Granny? Is it Ravyn?" I ask the question I know is also stuck in Theodora's throat.

"There is no doubt, though the monarchy is not admitting

that yet. Her minions came during the night; the Corrupted and her ravens killed, maimed, or blinded most of the Moonbright army. They are completely devasted. That is why there are messengers scattered about, seeking aid."

I do ask not the source of Granny's knowledge; Dionysia and her clan are the swiftest and most observant messengers of all, and the most trustworthy. I squeeze the bridge of my nose, sighing. "They have no idea what they are up against."

"Exactly. The king and queen refuse to leave the capital and go into hiding. Ravyn will strike there next to sow even more chaos, Lucien."

My head snaps up at this bit of information. Thea nudges me with her nose. She knows what I am worried about. "My parents haven't left? They do not even know I am still alive, and they will die because of their stubbornness before I can tell them I yet live!" My rage knows no bounds. I grit my teeth, clamping my fists. When will Ravyn ever stop her destruction? "Even the Moonbright mages will be no match for Ravyn Rathmore."

Theodora paws at my leg, then gazes west, toward Moonbright.

"You should stay here, Thea. I will go to Moonbright. I am heir to the kingdom, and I am duty bound to protect it." I kiss the top of her velvety muzzle, then turn to Granny, who stands still as a statue, blue eyes blazing. "I have healed and rested long enough, Granny. I am hale enough to travel. I can join the caravan from Murkfell. They will send at least one Red Cloak with them, so you do not have to worry about my health or wellbeing."

"That is not what I am worried about." Granny's eyes flick over to Thea. "She is not bound to one place, so you know she will follow you. Moonbright is her home too. And she needs to find Ravyn to break her curse. You may as well travel together, but you will have to be careful with Theodora in tow. Keep her safe from the trophy hunters."

Theodora paws at me again as if in agreement. I scratch the

top of her head and smile. I smile in spite of everything. The sun still shines, Theodora is still alive, and I am human again. All is not lost.

"Well, Theodora Mourningbeam, it looks like you will be my direwolf escort back to our home. Back to Moonbright. A new beginning for you and me, and for our people. But for Ravyn Rathmore, it is the beginning of the end."

ACKNOWLEDGMENTS

No book is complete without a village behind the author, so to the residents of my own Murkfell Village:

Thanks to my family for their unending support. Like Theodora to Lucien, you are always my light even in the darkest times; unending gratitude to my editor and friend S.R Malone, whose notes always bring clarity and purpose even through the murk (and thanks for voting on book covers!); and a huge thank you to fellow author and friend Chris Mason, who pumped me up many times to keep me going even when the path seemed dark. To my fellow Red Cloak witch Tilly McGill, whose beautiful art helped bring Lucien, Theodora, and the Murkfell Wood to life, I am eternally grateful. Blessed be, my friend.

And last but not least, I cannot forget to acknowledge my readers, including all the ones who read and commented on it in the early stages of its development. You are all stars in the Murkfell cosmos!

ABOUT THE AUTHOR

❧

H.R. Parker is an author, poet, and editor who hails from the coastal plains of Georgia. She has had over 100 poems and short stories featured in publications and anthologies such as *Writerly Magazine*, *Clover & Bee Magazine*, *AntipodeanSF*, and others. When she's not reading or writing, she's haunting graveyards, cuddling cute animals, or embracing her hobbit DNA and eating po-tay-toes. Find her work and socials at authorhrparker.com.

ALSO BY H.R. PARKER

Soul Harvest: A Novelette With Other Stories From the Cybervault

Paper Moon Sky: A Tiny Cosmic Poetry Collection

See my other published standalone works at www.authorhrparker.com

www.ingramcontent.com/pod-product-compliance
Lightning Source LLC
Chambersburg PA
CBHW011442170626
46807CB00009B/3280